John Nicholson

The martyrdom of Joseph Standing

The murder

John Nicholson

The martyrdom of Joseph Standing
The murder

ISBN/EAN: 9783337130763

Printed in Europe, USA, Canada, Australia, Japan

Cover: Foto ©Raphael Reischuk / pixelio.de

More available books at **www.hansebooks.com**

THE MARTYRDOM

OF

JOSEPH STANDING;

OR, THE

Murder of a "Mormon" Missionary.

A TRUE STORY.

ALSO

AN APPENDIX,

GIVING A

SUCCINT DESCRIPTION OF THE UTAH PENITENTIARY

*And some data regarding those who had, up to date
of this publication, suffered incarceration through the operations of the
anti-"Mormon" Crusade
begun in 1884.*

WRITTEN IN PRISON

BY JOHN NICHOLSON,

"A Convict for Conscience Sake."

SALT LAKE CITY, UTAH.
THE DESERET NEWS CO., PRINTERS.
1886.

PREFACE.

THE narrative which forms the principal feature of this little volume was penned under peculiar circumstances. Such a condition as privacy
has practically no existence in the Utah Penitentiary. The writing was therefore done by snatches,
in the midst of varied and almost incessant noises,
in the eating room, bunk-house or yard, as occasion presented or necessity demanded. This fact
should perhaps be a sufficient apology for any
defects it may contain. The story has one good
quality, however—it is strictly true. On that
ground it is with pleasure presented to the
public by

THE AUTHOR.

CONTENTS.

THE MARTYRDOM OF JOSEPH STANDING.

CHAPTER V.

CHAPTER VI.

APPENDIX.

CHAPTER I.

CHAPTER II.

CHAPTER III.

CHAPTER IV.

THE

Martyrdom of Joseph Standing;

OR, THE

MURDER OF A "MORMON" MISSIONARY.

CHAPTER I.

How the Story was obtained.—Rudger Clawson.—His Nativity, Appearance and Characteristics.—Conviction and sentence.—First Definition of "Unlawful Cohabitation."—Speech in Court.—Punished for Belief.—Prison Experience.

THE author was among the more early victims of the legal raid instituted against the Latter-day Saints under the "Edmunds Act," which prescribes penalties for polygamy and "unlawful cohabitation."

The rule in the courts has been, when a man has been placed in jeopardy for the latter offense, to inflict the full penalty, without reference to the character of the plea or other mitigating circumstances, unless he made a pledge to the judge in relation to his future conduct.

This promise, reduced to a plain statement of the situation, requires the person making it to repudiate a principle of his religion and cast a portion of his family adrift.

Such an agreement being at direct variance with our conceptions of duty, honor and integrity, we declined to be a party to it.

Having been previously convicted of "unlawful cohabitation" (living with and supporting our wives), we were, on the thirteenth day of October, 1885, sentenced by his honor, Chief Justice Zane, to imprisonment in the Utah Penitentiary for six months and to pay a fine of $300 and costs of the prosecution.   We entered the penitentiary the same day.

It is not the intention to present a relation of personal experience while in prison, but the foregoing brief preliminary statement is given simply by way of explanation as to how we obtained the particulars of the tragic story which constitutes the chief feature of this volume.

While a prisoner we had an excellent opportunity of becoming intimately acquainted with Rudger Clawson, whom we have learned to esteem and respect, on account of some sterling qualities he possesses.   Added to a sound understanding of the principles of the Gospel, he has an unusual degree of personal courage, both moral and physical, and integrity from which, up to this time, he has never swerved.

He was born in Salt Lake City, on the twelfth of March, 1857, an issue of plural marriage, being the son of Hiram B. Clawson and Margaret Gay Judd Clawson.

Rudger is slightly under medium height, and of stout build. His face is oval shaped and inclined to be plump. He has clear grey eyes; the nose is somewhat large, and has a tendency toward the Roman type; sufficiently so to give the impression of resoluteness. This feature gives a stronger intimation of firmness than the mouth, which is small, the lips being full and not usually closely compressed. Although he is in his thirtieth year, his appearance is more youthful than that age would generally denote.

He has been a subject of considerable interest in the community of Latter-day Saints and elsewhere, on account of being conspicuously connected with some circumstances of public prominence.

The case which culminated in his being sent to prison for a term of four years was the initiatory one under the Edmunds Act, consequently he was the first victim of the present anti-"Mormon" raid.

He was convicted of polygamy and unlawful cohabitation on the twenty-fifth day of October, 1884. On the first and more important count he was sentenced to imprisonment for three years and six months, and to pay a fine of $500, and on the second to be incarcerated for six months and to pay a fine of $300, the whole aggregating a penalty of four years and $800.

In charging the jury, Judge Zane gave his first definition of what constituted "unlawful cohabitation." He stated that in order to justify a verdict of guilty it was essential that the evidence should show a reasonable probability that there had been sexual commerce between the defendant and his plural wife. The flagrant manner in which he somersaulted from that position in order to insure convictions in subsequent cases is a matter of public notoriety.

When the judge asked the defendant on the day appointed for the judgment November 3, 1884, if he had anything to say why sentence should not be passed upon him, Rudger responded thus: "Your honor: Since the jury that recently sat on my case have seen proper to find a verdict of guilty, I have only this to say why judgment should not be passed upon me:

"I very much regret that the laws of my

country should come in conflict with the laws of God; but whenever they do, I shall invariably choose to obey the latter. If I did not so express myself I should feel unworthy of the cause I represent. The Constitution of the United States expressly provides that Congress shall make no law respecting an establishment of religion or prohibiting the free exercise thereof. It cannot be denied, I think, that marriage, when attended and sanctioned by religious rites and ceremonies, is an establishment of religion. The anti-polygamy law of 1862 and the Edmunds law of 1882 were expressly designed to operate against marriage as believed in and practiced by the Latter-day Saints. They are therefore unconstitutional, and, of course, cannot command the respect that constitutional laws would. That is all I have to say, your honor."

In the subsequent remarks of Judge Zane that official said that every man had the right to worship according to the dictates of his conscience, and to entertain any belief that his reason and judgment might dictate.

This was followed by this flat contradiction of his own theory:

"You violated it (the Edmunds Act), as you say, with the understanding that you had a right to

do so because there was a higher law by which
you govern your conduct. That being so, it
makes the case somewhat aggravated   *   *   *
I confess that I should have felt inclined to
fix the punishment smaller than I shall were it
not for the fact that you openly declare that you
believe it is right to violate the law, in that you
believe you are right in doing it."

Thus was the proposition that belief and worship were exempt from legal punatory process,
practically controverted by the judgment of the
functionary who expounded it. The defendant
received a heavier punishment on account of his
belief; consequently all that part of the penalty
that was in excess of what would bave been
inflicted in the absence of a certain belief was
imposed because of its presence in the mind of
the defendant.

It is no purpose of this sketch to describe the
disagreeable position in which Rudger Clawson
found himself during the first six months of his
incarceration, not only because of the ordinary
discomforts and inconveniencies of prison life, but
as well on account of the deep-seated and un-
reasonable prejudice that existed in the minds of
his fellow-convicts in relation to himself and the
Church with which he was identified. Among

the latter, however, he found a few friends, who stood by him in his isolation.

If any one wishes to witness the extremest forms in which human prejudice can find expression, they can be amply satisfied by residing for a time in this place of imprisonment. Then he could form some idea of the position in which Rudger was for a time placed, there being no soul of his own faith within those walls except Brother Joseph Evans, whose case was the next in order of date to his own. Those feelings of antipathy have gradually modified, however, until it has been supplanted by a sentiment of respect, and in many instances, even friendliness for most of the "Mormon" inmates of the penitentiary.

But it is not upon this phase of Brother Clawson's career that the writer proposes to dwell. It receives a merely incidental, or rather introductory mention. There is a thrilling chapter in his experience, the story of which has never been presented to the public in a connected and thoroughly intelligible form. It inculcates an event of momentous historical importance, being none other than the assassination, by a mob of religious fanatics, of Elder Joseph Standing, near Varnell's Station, Whitfield County, Georgia, on Sunday, July 21st, 1879. The chief reason for the penning of this sketch is that the details of that tragedy may be presented in a definite and consecutive shape.

CHAPTER II.

A Mission to Georgia.—A Dream and its fulfilment.—A tramp in the dark.—Entertained by Mr. Holston.—A sense of approaching Danger.

IN 1879, Rudger was called to go on a preaching mission to the Southern States, and proceeded to his field in the early part of that year. He labored in the State of Georgia, associated with Elder Joseph Standing. Before he reached that part of the country the latter had accomplished a good work in Whitfield County; particularly in the neighborhood of Varnell's Station, where he had succeeded in raising up a branch of the Church.

A short time before he was murdered, Brother Standing had a dream which made a powerful impression upon his mind, and caused him to have forebodings of approaching trouble. He told it to Rudger, and several times subsequently to other persons in his presence. It was about as follows, as near as his precise language can be recollected:

"I thought I went to Varnell's Station, when suddenly clouds of intense blackness gathered overhead and all around me. I visited a family who were connected with the Church. The moment I entered their house the most extreme consternation seized them, and they made it clear beyond any possibility of doubt that my presence was objectionable. They appeared to be influenced by a sense of great fearfulness. There was no clearing away of the clouds nor abatement of the restlessness of the people, when I suddenly awoke, without my being shown the end of the trouble."

In the meantime a conference was appointed to be held in Rome, Georgia, and Elders Standing and Clawson received an invitation to be present and participate in the proceedings. They accordingly set out on a journey to that point. Standing decided that a call should be made, on the way, at Varnell's Station, that they might visit some of the Saints, most of whom were new members of the Church. They reached that place on the evening of Saturday, July 9th, and proceeded to the residence of J———. As soon as they got to the house the inmates seemed to be in a state of great excitement. They said that threats had been made against the brethren, and the feeling toward them in the neighborhood was bitter and murderous. They declined to allow them to stop over night, because if anything happened they would have to share the trouble.

This reception chilled the feelings of the Elders, and Rudger said to himself involuntarily: "This is the fulfilment of Joseph's dream."

"What shall we do?" said the missionaries. "It is now nine o'clock, and getting quite dark. Can you tell us of a place where we can find shelter?"

"Yes," said J——, "you can go to Holston's, a mile and a half further on. He will doubtless entertain you."

There being no alternative, the two travelers left the house of the J——'s and set out for that of Henry Holston, who was not a member of the Church, but had shown a very friendly disposition toward the Elders. They trudged through the thickly wooded country, about one half of the way in pitchy darkness.

On reaching the Holston place, they discovered that the family had retired. In response to a knock, the voice of the proprietor was soon heard, saying, "Who is there?"

"Standing and Clawson," was the reply.

"Well?" said Mr. Holston, in that peculiar intonation that gave the impression that he was slightly hesitating about extending his hospitality.

The situation was briefly explained, the relation winding up with—"We would like the privilege of stopping over night."

The door instantly opened, and Mr. Holston said, with that cordiality for which he was noted, "Come in."

After the brethren entered he was very kind. He explained to them, however, that there was danger in the air. Threats of mobbing, whipping and even killing the Elders had been freely made, and he expected to get into trouble on account of entertaining them. He said, however, that he would take his chances on that head and would defend them so long as they were under his roof.

When the guests entered the room assigned them, Standing appeared pale, anxious and determined. It is not known whether his dream had occurred to him on account of the situation, as no expression from him denoted that such was the case. It was evident, however, that he was impressed with a premonition of approaching danger. He had always felt an intense horror of being whipped and more than once had declared that he would rather die than be subjected to such an indignity. Notwithstanding that he appeared to be deeply impressed with a sense of the near presence of danger, he was naturally a courageous young man.

He carefully examined the windows and securely fastened them. He then got hold of an iron bar, which he placed in such a position as to be within easy reach of his hand, in case of necessity.

"What is the meaning of these precautions?" said Rudger.

"I expect the mob to-night, and I want to be ready to receive them," was the resolute response.

"I don't think we will be disturbed," said the imperturbable Rudger, who forthwith fell into a sound slumber, from which he did not awake till broad daylight.

CHAPTER III.

Captured by a howling Mob.—Their brutal Threats and Conduct.—Standing's Manner and Expostulations.—Rudger receives a Blow.—Honest Owensby and his Horse.—A heroic Girl.—Scene of the Murder.—"Shoot that Man."—Horrible Spectacle.—"This is terrible."

EXT morning was the Sabbath, and the weather was clear and beautiful, all nature appearing to rest in peaceful serenity. The two Elders set out to go to the house at which they were received with such meagre hospitality the night previous, for the purpose of getting their satchels, etc., and bringing them on to Mr. Holston's place. They found the J———s still fearful because of the bitter feeling they knew existed in the neighborhood toward the brethren, and the stay of the latter was brief.

The road between J———'s and Holston's was densely wooded on both sides. On the way back to the residence of the latter, turning a bend the two young missionaries suddenly came in full view of a *posse* of twelve men. Some were mounted, the remainder were afoot and all were armed. As soon as they caught sight of the Elders they set up, unitedly, the most demoniacal

2

yells of exultation, and came rushing toward them like a pack of hungry wolves who had discovered the prey they were about to tear to pieces and devour.

The feelings that were inspired in Joseph Standing at this appalling spectacle can only be judged by his appearance. His face was pale as death, his features rigid, while his eye betokened the intensity of the subdued excitement under which he labored.

The sensations that passed through Rudger's mind and frame were entirely new to him, as he was now facing a danger that had no parallel in any former incident of his life, which he thought he was about to be compelled to surrender.

The names of those who composed this bloodthirsty band of murderous ruffians, whose cruel and dastardly deed will cause them to be branded with eternal infamy, are:

David D. Nations, Jasper N. Nations, A. S. Smith, David Smith, Benjamin Clark, William Nations, Andrew Bradley, James Faucett, Hugh Blair, Jos. Nations, Jefferson Hunter and Mack McLure.

The expressions upon the faces of those fiends incarnate were in unison with the vengeful sounds which had just escaped from their throats. They were laboring under the excitement of passion to such an extent that their frames shook and some of them foamed at the mouth.

As soon as they came up Joseph Standing, in a clear voice, loud enough to be heard by all of them, said:

"Gentlemen: By what authority are we thus molested upon the public highway? If you have a warrant of arrest or any other legal process to serve upon us, we would like to examine. it, that we may be satisfied as to your authority to interfere with our movements."

"We'll show you by what authority we act," some of them shouted.

One of the mounted mobbers then jumped from his horse and approached Rudger with a cocked revolver. He flourished this weapon, whirling it menacingly in the face of the young man, who looked down the muzzle of an implement of that character for the first time. It is perhaps needless to state that it looked exceedingly formidable to him. The murderous fellow who performed this part of the programme accompanied his threatening antics with the most foul and blasphemous abuse, while his companions were moving around and indulging in vile and profane cursings. The excitement of Bradley—a large and powerful man—was singularly noticeable. He was on horseback and was holding a double barrelled shotgun in front of him, across his animal, with both hands. He shook so that the weapon bobbed about as if he were about to drop it.

"Come with us," was the command from the mob.

The singular procession then started back in the same direction from which the Elders had come.

Standing appeared to be laboring under a terrible strain. His face continued overspread with a deathly pallor; he walked rapidly, and with his figure erect as an arrow. He moved so quickly that he kept pace with the front line of the mobbers, with whom he constantly reasoned and expostulated. "It is not our intention," said he "to remain in this part of the State. If we had been unmolested we would have been away in a very short time. We use no inducements to persuade people to join our Church. We preach what we understand to be the truth and leave people to embrace it or not, as they may choose," etc.

Such expostulations had not the slightest effect in mollifying the lawless band, but rather exasperated them all the more. Indeed it was not what the missionaries might do for which these base fellows had resolved to punish them, but for what had already been done, some of the best and most respected people in that section having embraced the gospel through Elder Standing's ministrations. They said: "The government of the the United States is against you, and there is no law in Georgia for Mormons."

. Rudger manifested no hurry in accompanying the gang. His overwhelming sentiment on that subject was one of reluctance. He could see no developments ahead but those of a most appalling character, and he was the reverse of anxious to hasten their consummation. He expected he was going to his death, and he had no desire to meet the grim monster any sooner than might be compulsory. He walked rather slowly, in order that he might not get too far ahead of his inclinations.

One of the ruffians, becoming exasperated at his tendency to lag, came up behind and struck him a terrible blow on the back of the head. Being stunned for the moment, Rudger reeled and fell forward, saving his body from the full shock of the fall by extending his hands. Recovering speedily, he was on his feet in an instant, his heart fired with consuming rage. He turned for the purpose of identifying his cowardly assailant, and found him to be a young man—probably the most youthful person of .the party. Rudger knew that to resent the brutal outrage would be certain and almost instant death. He looked at him, however, in such a manner as to convey all the contempt that could be indicated by facial expression.

This seemed to enrage the wretch almost as much as if he had received "blow for blow." Shortly after the helpless victim of his attack had resumed the melancholy line of march, the fellow assaulted him again. He raised a heavy club and was about to bring it down upon Rudger's head with all the force he was capable of using, when another member of the band seized his arm and told him to desist.

On proceeding a short distance further the party beheld a spectacle that, notwithstanding the serious character of the situation, caused some to show that they sensed its ludicrousness, by an involuntary smile. They came suddenly upon an old man, apparently about sixty years of age, mounted upon an alleged horse.

The name of this person was Jonathan Owensby. He was ponderous, even to hugeness, but not from excess of adipose. He was tall, rawboned, loose-jointed and sinewy. As he sat, or rather hung upon his horse, he reminded one of a bundle of knotty slabs. His face and head were large, and his complexion bordered upon the hue of tanned leather, the skin having a harmonious appearance of similar toughness. The features were large, projecting and craggy, the forehead receding with marked abruptness, leaving a jutting ledge, on the lower part, covered with a thick growth of shaggy hair, in the form of eye-brows, from under which peered a pair of poorly matched grey eyes. While the right optic gazed at you steadfastly the other seemed to be "taking in" the landscape on the left.

The animal upon which this peculiar person rode completed the picture. It looked as if nature had begun the work of making a horse and abandoned the job after having put the frame together.

Notwithstanding the forbidding character of Jonathan Owensby's personal appearance, his reputation for truthfulness and general honesty was second to none in the section of the country where he resided. A circumstance connected with the tragedy, the particulars leading to which are now being related, bore out the correctness of the estimate popularly placed upon the good man's character.

Addressing Jonathan, one of the mobbers said: "Is there anything the matter with your horse? If there is, these men are Elders of the 'Mormon'

Church, and will heal it by the laying ou of hands."

"I don't think there is anything the matter with him," said the old man, as he smiled grimly and passed on his way.

The party at this juncture turned out of the main road and went deeper into the woods. They had scarcely more than taken this change of route when they met a young girl named Mary Hamlin. It subsequently transpired that she and her mother, who were friendly to the Elders, had seen the mob and feared greatly that they might meet the brethren and kill them. At the suggestion of Mrs. Hamlin, her daughter set out to intercept the missionaries, put them on their guard and enable them to evade the mobbers. She was just a little too late, but it was no fault of this heroic girl, who had traveled with all the speed she could command.

When she comprehended the situation her face assumed a bleachy whiteness.

A terrible fear, combined with a determined resolution seized upon Rudger. Doubtless the mind of Brother Standing was similarly exercised. Knowing the unscrupulous characters of those who held the Elders in custody, an idea shot through his mind that they might commit an outrage upon the girl. In that event any attempt to prevent them consummating such a purpose would be certain death to himself and companion, yet he resolved to make it. Unarmed and helpless as he was, he purposed selling his life as dearly as possible, if need be, in defending this innocent young woman.

One of the men said: "You see we have got your brethren. As soon as we dispose of their case we purpose attending to you."

"The Lord is with them and my prayers are forever for them," replied Mary, the tones of her voice evincing deep emotion. She then went on her way.

At this juncture three of the members of the party who were on horseback left the main body and made a detour, probably to reconnoitre or to get others to join them in their villainous work.

The remainder, in charge of the two intended victims of their satanic hate, proceeded a short distance further, when they reached a lovely spot —a spring of clear water, overshadowed by a huge, outspreading tree. Here a halt was made and the party seated themselves around the mirror-like pool.

From the time the Elders were captured by the mob, Standing seemed to be affected with a burning thirst, probably occasioned by the suppressed excitement under which he was laboring. On the way he several times appealed to his captors for water, and now an opportunity was presented for the first time for him to obtain it.

One of the men, pointing to the spring, told him to drink.

The young man was furthest from the pool, and in order to reach it would have to pass close to several of the mobbers, and while reclining to reach the water would be an easy prey to any of the blood-thirsty crew who might take advantage of his prone position to do him violence. This probability appeared to flash across his mind, and he said: "I don't wish to drink now."

The man who told him to slake his thirst evidently divined what was passing through his mind, and said: "You needn't be afraid; you can drink, as we will not hurt you while you do so."

Standing went to the spring and took a copious draught. He was still very pale, his features rigid, and overspread with an expression of deep anxiety.

After he had returned to his place, James Faucett, aged about sixty years, and who was seated upon a horse, addressing the Elders, delivered himself as follows:

"I want you men to understand that I am the captain of this party, and that if we ever again find you in this part of the country we will hang you by the neck like dogs."

A general desultory conversation ensued, in the course of which the vilest accusations were laid against the "Mormons," the beastly talk of the mobbers merely serving to show the depravity and corruption of their own hearts. They betrayed a deep-seated hatred of Elder John Morgan. They were desirous of ascertaining his whereabouts from the Elders, and appeared disappointed on learning from them that he was at that time in Utah.

The space of about one hour was consumed in this way, when the three horsemen who had left the party came in sight. As they rode up, one of them exclaimed: "Follow us."

At this time Joseph Standing was sitting with his back toward the horsemen, but no sooner had the command embodied in the two words quoted been uttered than he leaped to his feet with a bound, instantly wheeled so as to face them, brought his two hands together with a sudden slap, and shouted in a loud, clear, resolute voice— "Surrender."

A man seated close to him pointed his pistol at

him and fired. Young Standing whirled or spun three times round upon his feet, fell heavily forward upon the ground, turned once over, bringing him face upward, and spread his arms widely out, his form being in such a position as to be in the shape of a cross.

As if moved by one impulse all those who had been seated upon the ground arose to their feet. Suddenly a member of the party, pointing to Rudger, said to his companions, in an authoritative tone—"Shoot that man."

In an instant, every weapon was turned upon the defenseless young missionary, who felt that his last moment on earth had come and that in a few seconds he would be launched into eternity. He fully realized the situation, his feelings being intensified by the expectation that a bullet was about to crash through his brain, the very idea of which had always been to him most horrible.

The murderous wretches paused a moment with their weapons leveled upon their proposed victim, who folded his arms—showing an outward calmness at the most extreme variance with his inward feelings—and said with apparent deliberation: "Shoot."

The suspense of a lifetime seemed to be thrown into the next few seconds. A whirling sensation passed over his brain and then all was dark. This condition was but momentary, and when he recovered the position was unaltered—the murderous ruffians still stood with their guns and pistols pointed at him. The man who had directed that the young Elder be murdered suddenly changed his mind and countermanded the first order by shouting "Don't shoot."

The men at once lowered their arms. They then appeared to sense the horrible character of the deed that had been committed. As soon as it flashed fully upon them, they were seized with sudden consternation and instinctively rushed together in a compact group, as if seeking mutual protection from each other, from the probable consequences of the bloody act.

Rudger walked over to where young Standing was lying, stooped and looked into his face. The spectacle that met his gaze sent a shock through his system that can never be erased from his memory. There lay his companion, recently in the full vigor of life and health—bright, capable and intelligent—in the throes of death. There was a large ghastly wound in the forehead, directly above the nose, the right eye had been torn out, the brain was oozing from the place where the bullet entered, and the death-rattle was sounding in his throat. Rudger gently raised the dying man's head and placed his hat under it to keep it out of the dust. He was then seized with a deep sense of grief, succeeded by a feeling of utter loneliness, which may well be imagined from the appalling character of the situation. Under the circumstances, he could but put his trust in God, who, for a wise purpose, had permitted one of His faithful servants to be brutally murdered.

As Rudger stood gazing at his friend and companion, he was approached by one of the Nations brothers, who said with a strong emphasis upon the last word of each exclamation: "This is terrible! This is terrible! This is terrible; that he should have killed himself in such a manner."

The missionary perceived the intention to resort to the suicide theory, and deeming it both imprudent and unsafe to openly repudiate it, replied: "Yes, it is terrible."

Then realizing the danger of giving the gang any time to sense the fact that to permit him to escape alive would be a menace to their safety, he saw there was no time to be lost.

He exclaimed: "Gentleman, it is a burning shame to leave a man to die in the woods in this fashion. For heaven's sake either you go and

procure assistance that the body may be removed
and cared for, or allow me to do so."
    He urged this point so earnestly and vehem-
ently that the gang consulted a moment and
then, turning to him, said: "You go."

CHAPTER IV.

A terror-incited Run.—A cold-blooded Woodchopper.—Rudger starts for Catoosa.—He confronts a startling Danger.
—What was done at Catoosa.—Significant Correspondence.—Holston visits the body.—A fresh horror for
Rudger.—The Inquest.

IT need scarcely be said that he did not wait
upon the order of his going, but went at
once. He felt that he had urgent business at a
convenient distance from that mob, and that he
could not breathe unrestrainedly while within
range of the villainous crowd.
    Before he could reach a wooded part of the
country it was necessary to cross an open space
extending a distance of about twenty rods.   He
had an almost uncontrollable desire to run, but
he dared not do so lest that course might cause
the lawless fellows to change their minds.   He

walked rapidly, however, yet it seemed to him like a journey of fifty miles. Every moment he was expecting to be shot in the back, and the relief he experienced when he reached cover is beyond the power of description.

As soon as he was out of the sight of the murderers, Rudger almost flew through the air. Urged on by a terrible desperation, his feet scarcely touched the ground as he placed the greatest practicable distance between himself and his enemies in the least possible time. The house of Mr. Holston, about two miles distant from the scene of the tragedy, was the objective point of the race he was running. When he had proceeded about a mile he heard a sound of chopping in the woods. It fell like sweet music upon his ear, as he thought it probably indicated the near proximity of some one who might prove "a friend in need"—a welcome change, in view of the experience of the last few hours.

He hailed the wood-chopper, by shouting "Halloo."

"Halloo," responded the axe-wielder. Rudger located the source of the sound, but was on the other side of a creek from the owner of the voice. Without seeing him he called to him in entreating tones: "A man has just been murdered in cold blood about a mile from here. Will you, for heaven's sake, go with me to the spot and assist in removing the body?"

After a pause came the heartless response: "No; I haven't time."

Rudger resumed his run for Mr. Holston's house, at which he soon afterwards arrived.

That gentleman had been informed by persons who had seen the armed mob that the lives of the Elders were in danger; he was therefore partially prepared for the tale of blood which was hurriedly related to him.

Said Rudger: "Will you go and look after the body while I go and obtain the services of a coroner?"

"Yes. I will go at once."

"Will you let me have the use of a horse?"

"Go to the stable and find an animal that will suit your purpose."

Mr. Holston then left for the scene of the assassination and Rudger started for Catoosa Springs, where the coroner resided, on horseback. ·

The road to Catoosa was lonely, that part of the country being but sparsely populated. Rudger put the animal on which he rode upon its metal. Doubtless it traveled at a speed that would have satisfied any ordinary, and even some extraordinary demands. To the impatient and overstrained mind of the rider it appeared like the progress of a snail compared with the rapidity with which he desired to go over the road. He reined up for a moment, procured·a club and with this pummeled the poor brute with it, in the desperate hope of urging him to a quicker gallop.

By the direct route from Holston's to Catoosa, the distance was about five miles, but owing to his being misdirected he got out of his way, making it seven miles by the route he took.

When about two miles from his destination, in turning a curve in the road he beheld a group of horsemen, numbering about six or seven approaching him from a distance. They appeared to be in a hurry, as they were traveling at a rapid rate.

When they came within about twenty rods of Rudger, he was confronted with a new and unexpected terror—he recognized them as members of the gang who murdered Elder Standing. He felt as if it would have been a relief for the earth to suddenly open and swallow him. He anticipated neither more nor less than that the wretches would assassinate him.

He could make a dash for cover, as the country was wooded, and thus have a chance, meagre though it might be, to escape.

No sooner had this idea flashed upon his mind than he abandoned it. He resolved to confront the danger, although it appeared to involve certain death. The condition of his mind at meeting, alone and defenseless, with those whose hands were reeking with the blood of his late companion, must be left to the imagination of the reader. It cannot be adequately delineated by the pen of mortal. The approaching party were all armed. The courageous young man rode forward. When he reached them, all reined up, and he fully anticipated being shot down. He expected no mercy.

"What have you done with Standing?" one of them exclaimed.

"I have not disturbed him, and I presume he lies just where he fell."

"Where are you going?"

Rudger extended his arm westward and, pointing with his index finger, said: "I am going in that direction."

Some of them smiled, and all rode on, their departure lifting a load from Rudger's mind that seemed like the removal of a mountain. It was also like a rift in the clouds of a day of gloom through which a cheering ray of light had brightly glinted.

The satisfaction of the mobbers at the answer given by Rudger as to where he was going, is easily explained. They imagined that he was fleeing from the country and was traveling in hot haste, in a terror-stricken state, for Utah. This was precisely the impression he wished to make upon them, and he misléd them by pointing toward Catoosa, which lay directly west from the point where he encountered the party.

His meeting with them was a cause for astonishment to him as well as terror. The reason for their presence at that point was, however, quite obvious. It was close to the line which separates Georgia from Tennessee, and they were making their way over the border into the latter State in order to evade pursuit and arrest for murder by the officers of the law.

Rudger pushed on to Catoosa, at which point he shortly arrived. His first object was to find the telegraph office, which was situated in the large hall of a capacious hotel.

He was begrimed and dirty with travel from head to foot, and his appearance upon the festive scene that the spacious apartment presented was extremely grotesque. The place was thronged with pleasure-seekers, dressed in the gay habiliments of fashion. Strains of lively music floated in the air while scores of people were whirling merrily in the mazy meshes of the dance.

But the appearance of the sad traveler was no more incompatible with the place and proceedings than the latter were to the feelings that possessed his soul. They seemed to him to be a hollow mockery of his condition. Perhaps the reader is more or less familiar with the sensation created in the human breast oppressed by some great grief occasioned by an irreparable loss, when some thoughtless or unimformed individuals break in upon his poignant reflections with bursts of rude and boisterous jocularity. If so, an approximate idea may be formed as to the effect produced upon the anxious traveler whose movements are now being traced, by the new surroundings into which he was suddenly precipitated.

The following dispatch was at once forwarded to the Governor of Georgia:

"CATOOSA SPRINGS, JULY 21ST, 1879.

"*Governor Colquitt, Atlanta:*

"Joseph Standing was shot and killed to-day, near Varnell's, by a mob of ten or twelve men.
"RUDGER CLAWSON."

The annexed was also sent at the same time:

"CATOOSA SPRINGS, GEORGIA,
       " JULY 21ST, 1879.

" *John Morgan, Salt Lake:*

"Joseph Standing was shot and killed to-day, near Varnell, by a mob of ten or twelve men. Will leave for home with the body at once. Notify his family.

                         "RUDGER CLAWSON."

It may appear to the reader that the dispatch to Governor Colquitt was not sufficiently detailed, and that there might be, in consequence, some danger of his misapprehending the character of the tragedy, Any idea of that kind will be at once dispelled by the following correspondence, which explains that Mr. Colquitt was not only familiar with Joseph Standing's identity, but also with the situation—as relating to anti-"Mormon" sentiments and proceedings—in Whitfield County:

       "VAN ZANT STORE,
          "FANNIN COUNTY, GA.,
              "JUNE 12TH, 1879.

"DEAR SIR:—As an Elder of the Church of Jesus Christ of Latter-day Saints, commonly called "Mormons," I take this occasion to address

a few lines to you as the highest officer of the
State.

"I have recently received several letters from
members of our denomination residing at Varnell
Station, Whitfield County, informing me that
Elders of my profession have been obliged at
times to flee for their lives, as armed men to the
number of forty and fifty have come out against
them, and have also on various occasions entered
their houses in search of said Elders.

"I am fully aware, dear sir, that the popular
prejudice is very much against the "Mormons,"
and that there are minor officers who have apparently winked at the condition of affairs above
referred to.   But I am also aware that the laws of
Georgia are strictly opposed to lawlessness and
extend to her citizens the right to worship God
according to the dictates of conscience.

"History, however, repeats itself, and the laws,
where prejudice exists, are not always executed
with impartiality.

"A word or line from the Governor would undoubtedly have the desired effect. Ministers of
the Gospel could then travel without fear of being
stoned or shot and the houses of the Saints would
not be entered in defiance of all good law and
order.

"Your kind attention to this matter will be duly appreciated by

"Your humble and obedient servant,

"JOSEPH STANDING,

"*Presiding Elder of the Georgia Conference.*

"To His Excellency, Governor Colquitt, Atlanta, Ga."

"ATLANTA, GA., JUNE 21ST, 1879.

"*Mr. Jos. Standing, Van Zant Store, Ga.:*

"DEAR SIR:—In reply to your letter of the 12th inst., the Governor directs me to say that your statement is entirely correct, that 'the laws of Georgia are strictly opposed to all lawlessness,and extend to her citizens the right of worshiping God according to the dictates of conscience.'

"Under the provisions of our State constitution, the reformation of religious faith or of opinion on any subject, cannot legitimately be the object of legislation, and no human authority can interfere with the right to worship God according to the requirements of conscience. So long as the conduct of men shall conform to the law, they can not be molested and even for non-conformity thereto they can be interfered with only as the law may direct. No individual or combin-

ation of individuals can assume to vindicate the
law. Courts and juries are instituted for that
purpose, and to them alone is committed the office
of legally ascertaining the perpetrations of crime,
and of awarding punishment therefor.

"The Governor regrets to hear the report you
give from Whitfield County. He will instruct
the State prosecuting attorney for that district to
inquire into the matter, and if the report be true,
to prosecute the offenders. I am, sir,

"Very respectfully yours,

"J. W. WARREN,

"*Secretary Executive Department.*"

So far as known, the Governor, in the period
intervening between the date of his reply to
Elder Standing's letter and the tragedy, had
failed to fulfill his promise to take steps toward the
enforcement of the law against mobocracy in
Whitfield County.

After the coroner had been notified of what
had occurred, that official, his clerk and Rudger,
set out for Mr. Holston's place, where they
arrived at about five o'clock in the evening.

Mr. Holston then related to them the following
particulars:

"At the same time as Elder Clawson left for

Catoosa, I set out for the scene of the assassination, and found Standing lying in his blood. I examined the wound, and while doing so I discovered that the young man was not yet dead. I made another discovery that caused me to fear every moment that I would be murdered myself, as I was unarmed, and consequently not in a position to defend myself. I saw armed men—members of the party who committed the murder—loitering about the edge of the adjacent woods, closely watching my movements. Notwithstanding the alarm I naturally felt under the circumstances, I remained a sufficient length of time to enable me to construct a shade of bows to shelter the body from the scorching rays of the sun, the weather being extremely hot. After having performed that office, being about all I could do under the circumstances, I returned home."

A little party, consisting of the coroner and clerk, Rudger, Mr. Holston and four or five others proceeded to the spot where the murder was committed. When they reached it the sun was setting, and a group of awe-stricken and silent people were standing around Brother Standing's body. It was a solemn and impressive scene.

Rudger involuntarily approached the corpse

and discovered that some one had taken the hat
from under the head and placed it over the face
of the dead. He removed this temporary cover-
ing and looked into the now inanimate countenance of his late companion and friend. His eyes
were saluted with a fresh horror. The fiends
incarnate who had slain an innocent and unof-
fending man in cold blood had not been satisfied
with inflicting a simple death wound. While he
lay there in his blood and the cold grasp of death,
they had approached their victim and shot into
one side of his face and neck until they were
fairly riddled with bullets. Those who discharged
the weapons used for this atrocious work must
have stood directly over the body, the parts in
which the leaden messengers were buried being
powder-burnt.

On first reflection the theory that suggests itself
as to the incentive that led to this barbarous
climax to a bloody outrage is that the perpetrators were inspired with unmitigated satanic hate
that reached beyond this life and stepped into the
precincts of death. Bad and depraved as these
wretches were, such an explanation is probably
incorrect. The first mortal wound was inflicted
by one member of the party. Yet all were acces-
sory to, before and after the fact. It is not unusual

for men who commit a common crime to enter into compacts to stand by each other for mutual protection against the just reward of their deeds. It is likely therefore that those men agreed to stand upon an undoubted common ground in regard to the assassination of Joseph Standing, and to make the obligation and understanding complete each actually fired into the person of the victim.

A jury was empanelled on the spot and an inquest held by the coroner. The testimony of Rudger Clawson, Henry Holston and others was taken. It was on information imparted by Mr. Holston and some others who testified that the names of the actual murderers were obtained. This enabled the jury to return a clearly defined verdict, which was to the effect that the deceased came to his death by twenty gunshot wounds, inflicted by means of weapons in the hands of the twelve men whose names are given near the beginning of this narrative.

CHAPTER V.

A Friend in need.—A sad Procession.—Rudger's melancholy Task.—Arrival of the Officers of the Law.—Difficulties met in preparing the Body for transportation.—The arrival Home.

HEN the inquest was concluded, a momentous question was broached by the coroner he said: "What is to be done with the body?" Not a soul responded, and an unbroken silence pervaded the party for several minutes. No one appeared willing to take the risk of becoming by the performance of a humane and friendly act, a probable victim of anti-"Mormon" hate and vengeance. It was a trying and critical moment for poor Rudger, who stood apparently alone and friendless in a strange country, under circumstances of a most perplexing as well as sorrowful character. Of course he could say nothing.

There was one man who had stood by him thus far. Had his friendship faded? As this reflection passed through Rudger's mind that same person—the noble and generous-hearted Holston—broke the stillness and said: "Take the body to my house."

A large, wide plank was procured from an adjacent deserted cabin. Upon this the corpse was laid. Four pieces of wood were placed under the board, so that eight men could carry the inanimate burden. Rudger, the coroner and Mr. Holston were among the pall-bearers who carried this rude, extemporized bier. The others were promiscuous persons who had gathered to the spot from curiosity.

By the time the sad procession were ready to march through the woods it was dark. They had moved but a short distance until the gloom was impenetrable. There was no symptom of a breeze; not even enough to stir a leaf. Nothing was heard but the dull tramp, tramp, tramp of the bier-bearers, and the resounding echo of their foot-falls, which were necessarily regular to maintain the balance of the burden. The sombre nature of the whole incident was painful in the extreme, and especially so to him who was helping to bear the body of his murdered friend, brother and companion.

This monotonous gloom was suddenly relieved by the human voice. The coroner addressed Rudger: "What disposition do you propose to make of the corpse?"

"I intend to take it home to Utah."

"I think such an idea is preposterous. I do not believe you could find a railway company who would give you transportation for it, and even if you did they would probably throw it off somewhere on the road. It appears to me that the better way would be to bury the body here, and then, in the course of two or three years, the bones could be taken up and removed to any point that might be desired."

"I view the matter quite differently," was the resolute response. "I feel that the spirit of Elder Standing would never be satisfied to have his body buried where he was murdered. He would prefer it to be laid away in the land where his friends and kindred dwell. I should feel so if I were in his place, and I intend doing in regard to him as I would wish should be done by me under similar circumstances."

This ended the conversation, and the bearers of the body soon reached Mr. Holston's house.

A rude support was constructed in the front yard of the premises, and on this the plank upon which the body lay was placed.

At this juncture a new difficulty presented itself—no person present knew anything about preparing a corpse for the casket. In this dilemma Rudger, who had never had the slightest experience in that line, was under the necessity of undertaking the task.

A tallow candle was procured and placed near the head of the body. A vessel of warm water was brought and with these materials and some cloths Rudger proceeded with the melancholy and distressing work before him. It was a difficult duty, as the blood that had flowed from the wounds was spread over the head, face and neck of the corpse and had dried into a thick crust, the hair being all clogged and matted. This labor of love and friendship occupied a full hour, the operator receiving no assistance or aid from the group of curious on-lookers, who stood around and gazed upon the weird spectacle.

The scene must be largely left to the imagination of the reader. Its constituents were unique as well as solemn. The deepest silence prevailed, the intense darkness was only relieved by the dull rays of a tallow candle, whose dim flicker revealed the ghastly face of the dead, and the sad and earnest countenance and form of the young man who was performing some of the last offices of affection for his deceased friend. The awe-stricken spectators who were thrown into partial relief by the subdued light of the sickly dip. The huge trees, though scarcely perceptible, formed a fitting frame to the gloomy picture. Added to this were the furtive and fearful glances cast by the people into the dense darkness beyond, as if they anticipated that at any moment the quiet of the place might be suddenly interrupted by an incursion of blood-thirsty anti-"Mormon" mobocrats.

Finally Rudger's dreary task was finished, the body being washed, and clothed in clean gar-ments. A sheet was thrown over the corpse and all retired into the house.

About this time the sheriff of Whitfield Coun-ty, accompanied by a deputy and *posse*, arrived from Dalton, a town of 9,000 inhabitants, dis-tant about twelve miles. This officer was a tall, sinewy man, of tawny complexion. His hair was turning grey, and he had the appearance of a person of about fifty years of age. He was ex-ceedingly demonstrative and made strong pro-fessions of interest in Rudger. To the latter this was quite refreshing, because it was something new, for even Mr. Holston was not loud in his manifestations of friendliness. His friendship was evinced by acts more than words. Alto-gether Rudger thought the sheriff a pretty good fellow, but was not favorably impressed by his, deputy, a short, dumpy man, approaching middle age, who was quite reserved.

4 .

Said the sheriff: "Mr. Clawson, I very much regret that such a cold-blooded murder should have occurred in *my* county. I can assure you that every possible effort will be made to capture the perpetrators and bring them to justice."

The officer was informed of the fact that seven of the assassins had been seen traveling with hot haste toward the Tennessee border.

The *posse* then left, and, as it was approaching midnight, Rudger retired to rest after passing through an experience in one brief day that has but few parallels in individual history. He slept in undisturbed soundness until the blaze of the following day had appeared in the full flush of its brilliance.

A cursory examination revealed the fact that Elder Standing's body had begun to decompose. Rudger at once set out for Dalton to obtain a metallic casket. He had on a former occasion visited that place in còmpany with his late deceased companion, the news of whose assassination was now well known throughout the town. It caused a profound sensation, and Rudger, being recognized, was a centre of attraction and curiosity. He was plied with questions and advice on every hand. He was advised strongly not to return to the vicinity of Varnell's to get

the body, as those who thus counseled him believed if he did his life would be taken. The
reply to all this was that he should go in any
event, no matter as to the risk he might run.

Rudger had no money, but the undertaker let
him have the casket, and forwarded it by conveyance to Holston's, he taking the young man's
word that he would obtain means for payment
within a few days. Accordingly he telegraphed
to Benedict, Hall & Co., of New York, for $200,
which was promptly furnished, with an assurance
from that firm that they could be commanded
for any further amount that might be needed.

Rudger, accompanied by an employe of the
undertaker's, followed the casket in a buggy. On
the way he related the circumstances of the murder to his companion. He soon questioned his
own prudence in doing this, as the narrative so
excited that individual that he became almost
panic-stricken. Every now and then he would lean
out of the vehicle and peer into the woods and
along the road. He seemed to take every clump
for a group of anti-"Mormon" mobbers in ambush, and each bare and projecting limb of a
blighted tree seemed in his eyes to take the form
of a shotgun. His exclamations erstwhile were
in unison with his movements.

Holston's was reached at about five o'clock in the evening. The body was soon enclosed in the metallic casket, and the undertaker's employe left for the place from whence he came.

Next morning it was discovered that a fearful stench emitted from the casket, not only showing that decomposition was advancing rapidly, but also that the case was not hermetically sealed. This necessitated the conveyance of the body to Dalton for re-enclosure. To accomplish this the services of a team, wagon and driver and a couple of scouts, were engaged. The latter were on foot and walked about ten or fifteen rods ahead of the wagon containing the corpse. Rudger rode on the vehicle in company with the driver.

The employment of scouts was a precautionary measure against a sudden surprise, as the road to Dalton passed through Varnell's Station, the vicinity where Standing's murderers resided.

When within about half a mile of Varnell's, Rudger said to the teamster:

"Are you armed?"

"Yes," was the meek response, the driver at the same time producing from the pocket of his coat a very innocent-looking weapon in the shape of a pistol a few inches long, of the pepper-box pattern, and of an antiquated appearance generally.

The harmless aspect of this article, which was barely entitled to be designated a firearm, caused Rudger to smile. Being the most formidable weapon within reach, however, he borrowed it, got out of the wagon and tramped through the woods, so as to give Varnell's as wide a berth as practicable, while the team went straight on. Notwithstanding the puny character of the pepper-box, in making that circuit he derived some comfort from its temporary possession, and marched along with it in his hand, cocked and ready for action.

Dalton was reached in safety. The undertaker, instead of removing the body from the case in which it was enclosed, simply made a very large one, placed the other in it and filled the intervening space with cinders and dust from a locomotive. This material being heavy, the combined weight of the body and casing was thus increased to nearly nine hundred pounds.

In this shape the corpse was conveyed by rail to Utah, where Rudger arrived in charge of it on the first day of August, 1879. The news of the tragedy had created a deep sensation in the community of Latter-day Saints. At Ogden a brass band, an organized body of members of the Young Men's Improvement Associations, and a multitude of other people awaited the arrival at the depot of that town. In Salt Lake also a concourse of people had assembled at the Utah Central railway station. By the time Rudger and his sacred charge reached that point, however, night had cast its sombre mantle over the city of the Saints, and the body of the youthful martyr was taken directly to the office of Sexton Taylor.

The obsequies were conducted in the Tabernacle on Sunday, August 3d, in the presence of about 10,000 people. The speakers on the occasion were President John Taylor and President George Q. Cannon.

The body was interred, in the Salt Lake City cemetery, the same day.

CHAPTER VI.

Rudger returns to Georgia in the capacity of a Witness.—Holston's Peril.—How the Murderers were captured.—The Trial. — Attendant Circumstances.—The Result.—Rudger returns Home.—Memento of the young Martyr.

AFTER Rudger had been at home about eight months, he received a subpœna issued by the Circuit Court of Whitfield County, Georgia, requiring him to appear at Dalton the

following October (1880), and testify in the cases
of Jasper N. Nations, Andrew Bradley and Hugh
Blair, charged with the killing of Joseph Standing.

He consulted with President John Taylor, who
informed him that as he was the person who
would have to assume any personal risk that
might be involved in the matter, he desired him
to go or not, as he might elect. He decided to
respond to the subpœna, independent of any
regard for his personal safety.

Accordingly he made his appearance in Dalton
in September, 1880, where he was joined by Elder
John Morgan, the President of the Southern
States Mission.

He found the feeling amongst the populace of
that place to be exceedingly bitter, there being
imminent danger of an outbreak of open hostility.
He had a duty to perform, however, and he was
determined to accomplish it, so that the people
of the State of Georgia might not have it to say
that the murderers of Elder Standing went unwhipped of justice because the prosecuting witness had failed to do his part in the premises.

At Dalton, Rudger met with his friend Henry
Holston. He had previously informed that gentle-
man that he would return and attend the trial.
He never forgot that declaration. Numbers of

men, on account of the inimical feeling that had been worked up against Rudger, declared he would never come back. Holston always expressed his confidence that he would, however, although one man offered to bet him fifty dollars and another a horse that he was mistaken. As may be imagined, he was exceedingly pleased to find his expectation vindicated.

In the meantime, Mr. Holston had passed through a trying ordeal, which may as well be told, as near as can be, in his own words.

He said to Rudger:

"After you left, the whole community where I lived turned against me, so that it appeared as if I had no friends. Those who may have been kindly disposed were afraid to exhibit that feeling, because of the danger of their incurring the same hatred to which I was subjected. My life has been threatened over and over again, and I know that the friends of the men who murdered Standing thirst for my blood.

"I have been constantly on the watch, and one of the first things I did was to increase my weapons of defense. In addition to my gun, I procured a brace of Colt's navy revolvers, because I knew that the mobbers might attack my place any night.

"It was well that I took these precautions. One very dark night I went to a window and looked out. I saw, close to the gate that leads into the yard, a man on horseback, silent and motionless. I knew he was not alone, and was well aware of the purpose of the visit. There is no doubt in my mind that there were other nocturnal visitors, at a convenient distance, in ambush. I did not hesitate about the course I should pursue. I placed my revolver at full cock, then brought my watch-dog, a large, faithful animal, to my side. Quick as a flash, I opened the door. The dog bounded through the opening, flew down the path and made a spring at the horseman. The brute barely missed his aim.

"In the meantime, I was not idle. Following close upon the heels of the dog I ran toward the gate, firing rapidly at the retreating prowler, who sped with all the fleetness possible until the sound of his horse's hoofs ceased to fall upon the ear. I knew that he and his companions—whoever they were—would trouble me no more that night, as they were doubtless much more scared than I was.

"If that dog had got a hold on that fellow he never would have let go. He would have dragged him to the earth and I would have done the rest.

I should certainly have killed him. I would have been vindicated in doing so, as there is a law of Georgia which protects a person who slays another under circumstances of that character.

"I know that my life is in danger, and if any of these men come upon my premises I shall shoot them down like dogs."

No one who might hear his recital, see his gleaming eyes as he spoke, and observe the manner in which he—according to his habit when speaking resolutely—pushed the fingers of his right hand through his sandy hair, making it stand erect and causing it to add to the fierceness of his aspect, had any reason to doubt his assertion. He was known to be courageous and determined, and doubtless his enemies were afraid of him. Had it not been for those characteristics he would probably not have been alive to tell of this night adventure. He said, however, that his position was so unsafe that he would be obliged to leave that part of the country, and it is understood that he subsequently did so.

It was stated in an earlier part of this narrative that Rudger was favorably impressed with the sheriff of Whitfield County, but felt otherwise regarding his more undemonstrative deputy.

He met the latter at Dalton, and according to

a statement made by him the estimate of the relative character of the two men was incorrect.

It often occurs in life that men who boast the most about their capabilities and intentions show to the least advantage when it comes to actual work. These loud individuals are, as a matter of course, too frequently measured from the basis of their pretentions. The consequence is that the estimate is generally much more capacious than the article to which it refers. On the other hand those who are reticent about what they are capable of and purpose doing are the men to act in an emergency. Yet their modesty, exhibited ahead of the attainment of any specified undertaking, occasionally causes them to be placed below par in comparative estimation.

The story told by the deputy regarding the capture of the three murderers shortly to be put on their trial was not only related with unequivocal directness, but no circumstance subsequently learned appeared in the least degree to tarnish its truthfulness. It is herewith given, as related by the officer:

"When the sheriff, myself and *posse* left Holston's on the night of the day that Standing was murdered, we had gone but a short distance when the chief officer of the party said to me: 'I guess

we had better give up the idea of hunting the
men who killed Standing. The man they murdered was only a 'Mormon,' and it doesn't matter
about the perpetrators being brought to justice.'"

"I replied: 'On the contrary I think it matters
a great deal, and if you do not pursue those men
and do all in your power to arrest them I shall
report you to the court.'

"This had the effect of intimidating the sheriff.
We traveled all that night, going over the border
into Tennessee, and all the next day. In the
evening we came in sight of an isolated house,
and satisfied ourselves, by indisputable evidence,
that some of the men we wanted were within.
We took no immediate steps, but surrounded the
house and waited till next morning.

"At daylight a member of our *posse* was sent to
the door to demand the surrender of the men we
were after. A woman appeared, she denied that
they were there. She was told, however, that we
knew they were secreted in the house, and that if
they did not come out the *posse* would fire into
the building.

"This had the desired effect, for in a short time
Andrew Bradley, Jasper N. Nations and Hugh
Blair came out and surrendered.

"The news of the capture spread through the

neighborhood like wild-fire, and in a short time a crowd collected, the people coming from every direction. They were greatly excited, and threats of a rescue were made. We were told that we would never reach the jail with the prisoners.

"The sheriff was overawed and passive, and the situation critical. I was forced, under the circumstances, to assume the lead.

"'You shall see whether we will take them to jail,' I exclaimed.

"We placed the three prisoners on as many horses. This done they were brought close together, abreast. We then took a chain and fastened it around the neck of each, by means of looping, secured by padlocks.

"Turning to the threatening crowd, I said: We shall take these men to prison or they shall die. The first movement toward their rescue shall be the signal for us to shoot them down, and after that we will fight for our lives.

"We then started for Dalton, and having necessarily to travel slowly, were a considerable time on the way. We reached there without being molested, however, although the chances appeared strong when the capture was made that there would be trouble and bloodshed.

"Shortly after they were placed in jail, the prisoners were released on furnishing bail to the amount of $5,000 each."

Rudger met the three murderers several times on the streets. He recognized them at once as members of the gang who committed the bloody crime. Nations was about thirty-five years old, tall, dark and swarthy, and wore a pointed black beard. Bradley was aged about forty-eight years and of heavy build. He had a broad face and large nose, being altogether a coarse and brutal appearing specimen of humanity. Blair was aged about thirty years, and had a boyish, immature appearance.

Elder Clawson went before the grand jury and told the story of the murder. Henry Holston, Mary Hamlin and Jonathan Owensby also testified before the same body. The result was that the three men accused were indicted on three counts—murder in the first degree, manslaughter, and riot. The reason for this tripartite action was that, in case the defendants should be acquited on the most serious charge, they might be convicted of one of the others.

The finding of a true bill in the case caused considerable surprise, as it was popularly expected that the charges would be ignored.

Rudger and Elder Morgan had an interview

with Solicitor-General A. T. Hackett, in charge of
the prosecution. That officer seemed to be fair-
minded and expressed his purpose to use every
legitimate effort to bring the murderers to justice.
The brethren also secured the services in behalf
of the prosecution, of Col. W. R. Moore, an attorney of established ability.

Five attorneys were engaged on the side of the
defense.

In a few days the trial of Jasper N. Nations was
begun, Judge McCutchen, a gentleman about sixty
years old, and somewhat similar in personal
appearance to Judge C. S. Zane, was on the bench.

Considerable time was consumed in procuring
a jury. About one hundred and fifty men were
examined before a full panel was obtained. The
difficulty arose from a general reluctance to serve
on the case. Notwithstanding the popular feeling
in favor of the accused, doubtless it was widely
believed they were guilty. The disinclination~to
sit on the jury was evidently caused by the fact
that the position presented a probable dilemma,
neither horn of which was attractive. To decide
against the accused—should the evidence warrant
it—would subject the jury to a storm of popular
anger; to find, in that situation, in favor of the
defendants and thus act in opposition to the law

and the facts would place a man in whom there existed a scintilla of conscience, in an unpleasant position. To avoid either contingency the worming-out process on various subterfuges was liberally resorted to.

When the panel of twelve men, supposed to be "góod and true," was filled, a glance sufficed to create the impression that the box included a very hard-looking set.

In cases involving the guilt of three or more persons, the law of Georgia allows a separate trial to each, should he so elect, and the introduction of the other accused persons as witnesses. This line of action was adopted by the defendants, and Jasper N. Nations was first placed on trial on the count of the indictment charging murder in the first degree.

The interest in the case was so intense that it was said to be unparalleled in that part of the country. As a consequence the court-room was crowded to excess during each session.

Among the five lawyers engaged on the defense was a young attorney named Williamson. He was unusually tall and slender. He was fair, with light hair and a moustache of similar hue. He seemed to be as dotingly fond of the latter article as the average maiden lady of uncertain

age is of a favorite cat, and as frequently caress-
ingly stroked it.

This was his first case, as he was just launch-
ing out into the troubled sea which opens up to
the ambitious youth who aspires to such legal
honors as were attained by a Blackstone, a Mar-
shall or a Black. He was evidently inflated at the
sudden prominence in which he found himself.
He assumed a look of solemn gravity, and made
himself what is vulgarly called "numerous," to
the no small amusement of some of the spectators
shrewd enough to penetrate the flimsy crust of
ostentation in which the deluded young man envel-
oped himself.

He was full of suggestions, and kept stretching
his neck, *a la* crane, to catch with nice accuracy
some statement that was being made. Then he
would lean over the table and whisper, with an
air of mystery, some supposed important hint to
associate counsel. Following up this line of action he would express himself openly upon some
point with a manner which indicated that when
he ventured upon an elucidation it ought to be the
end of controversy. Then he would walk over to
where some member of the bar was seated and
make some facetious confidential remark, producing a mechanical smile upon the face of his

5

listener, who evidently supposed he was expected to indicate that he had heard something which embodied a vein of humor. Then the young fellow would stride to and fro across the bar with his hands deep down in his breeches pockets, except when one was occasionally withdrawn in order to pass it through his hair, to make it stand up and give the person whose head it adorned a more severely intellectual appearance, his eye-brows being meanwhile knitted after the manner of a man contemplating a difficult problem for the purpose of clearing up its more mysterious depths.

To the reader who has frequented the Third Judicial District Court of Utah, this picture will not appear to be over-drawn, for there occasionally has its counter-part been presented. We have seen it several times repeated.

While the trial was in progress the editor of the Atlanta *Constitution*, one of the most influential papers published in Georgia, paid a personal visit to Dalton, for the express purpose of getting a clear statement of the facts. He secured the assistance of Mr. Williamson, the young attorney, who was not only willing but eager to write an article on the subject. He did so and placed it in the hands of the editor.

The latter called at the hotel where Rudger and Elder Morgan were stopping and handed to them Williamson's statement, at the same time ·giving them the privilege of correcting any inaccuracies that it might embody and of making any additions that they might, from their knowledge of the facts, deem necessary.

This offer was gladly accepted, as the statement was discolored, distorted and altogether far from being fair. It was specially penned so as to favor the defendants. Misstatements were corrected and additions made, and by the time it passed into the hands of the editor again it was pretty thoroughly metamorphised, and presented a fair and just elucidation of the tragedy, and facts connected with it.

Next day Mr. Williamson carried the indisputable appearance of a man laboring under an attack of abstraction. His mind was evidently not on the case in progress. He was restless and anxious. There was something that he esteemed to be weighty resting upon his mind. The fact is he was impatiently looking for the arrival of the latest issue of the Atlanta *Constitution.* He cast occasional furtive glances toward the door, and at last he was relieved by the appearance thereat of the festive newsboy. He darted toward

him, secured a copy, plunged into a chair and be-
gan the perusal of his alleged article.

These movements were watched with some
amusement by Rudger. The reader of the paper
appeared to get along well enough until he
reached a point below the first paragraph, when
his face became clouded. As he progressed the
facial darkness deepened. He cast a half-inquir-
ing, half-indignant glance at Rudger, but the latter
was looking innocently into space, as if oblivious
to any of his surroundings. He then put the
paper down a moment; took it up again; read a
little more; made a remark to a brother attorney, and finally gave up the perusal of the
sheet with a look of disgust, being the effect of
the conclusion he had by this time reached—
that the editor of the *Constitution* evidently had
neither confidence in his veracity nor his literary
ability.

The reason why the editor submitted Williamson's article to Rudger and Elder Morgan for
revision and correction was ascertained by them.
Certain scandalous statements in reference to
Joseph Standing had appeared in the *Constitution*
some months before the murder. The editor
subsequently discovered that they were totally
untrue and he took this course for the purpose of

atoning in some degree for the injury he had inadvertently done to an innocent man.

Returning to the trial, Rudger was the first and principal witness and told a straight story of the tragedy, and the main facts connected with it.

When under examination by the attorneys for the defense he was subjected to the most disgraceful brow-beating. They forced him to repeat different portions of his statement over and over again, in the hope of entrapping him in a contradiction. They attributed assertions to him that he never made, and resorted to every subterfuge they could think of in order to find an excuse for impeaching his testimony and finally proceeding against him for perjury. They were baffled, however, at every turn, as his original statements were time and again repeated not only in substance, but as near as possible in the same language.

The judge throughout showed his bias in favor of the defense, and failed to protect the witness. He almost invariably decided in favor of that side, in points of dispute where a judicial ruling became necessary. There was one point, however, in which he took the opposite course. The defendant's attorneys introduced a great deal of irrelevant matter, especially with regard to the

"Mormon" Church. The object of this was to prejudice the jury against the prosecution and in favor of their client. One question asked the witness was—"Are your parents living in the practice of polygamy and are you a polygamous child?"

The witness declined to answer, and, remarkable to relate, the court overruled the interrogation as improper.

When an attorney for the defendant was cross-examining Rudger in reference to his original statement, he asked him what was said at a certain stage of events preceding the killing. The witness replied: "A member of the gang said: 'The government of the United States is against you and their is no law in Georgia for Mormons.' Judging from the manner in which this trial is being conducted I see no reason to question the correctness of his assertion."

This retort produced a brief suspension in the proceedings, which were, however, shortly resumed without the "soft impeachment" meeting with a rebuke.

Henry Holston and Mary Hamlin testified to the facts connected with the case of which they were cognizant, as heretofore related in this sketch, each telling a direct and truthful story.

Much importance was attached to whatever might be obtained from Jonathan Owensby. It was regarded, owing to the reputation for truthfulness of that worthy man, that whatever he might say would be as good as gospel. So it was. His evidence was in unison with his prominent trait. The precision with which he narrated every detail connected with his meeting the mob with the Elders in charge, in the woods, the remarks made on the occasion, the identity of the members of the gang, the manner in which they were armed, etc., showed that in addition to a clear conscience, the old man possessed a retentive memory and fair powers of observation.

The prosecution being closed, Andrew Bradley was placed on the stand for the defense.

He was asked to explain how it was that he was found armed and in company with a number of other men in the same condition, on the day of the murder:

He said: "I concluded that I would go hunting turkeys, that being the business I was engaged in on that occasion. I could not explain how it was that I fell in with those other men." _

This deep and lucid explanation doubtlesss had great weight with the jury, judging from the result of the trial. Its effect was perhaps heightened by the fact that Bradley was traveling along the main road, which wild turkeys have sufficient sense of self-protection to carefully avoid.

Hugh Blair was also introduced and testified. He was asked the same question. He said: "My gun was out of order and I started from my place to go to the premises of my brother-in-law, a short distance away. He kept a blacksmith's shop and I was going to get him to repair my gun. It was while I was on the way that I met those men."

This statement was equally as satisfactory as that given by Bradley, especially when it is taken in connection with the fact that the murder was committed on the sabbath, when all blacksmiths' and other shops are closed and work in them suspended. That part of Blair's proceeding in changing his alleged original intention of having his gun repaired on a certain Sunday, and accompanying a band of armed men and taking part in a cold-blooded murder was very prudently ignored.

This comprised the testimony for the defense, while that given for the prosecution was not only direct but overwhelming.

Solicitor-General Hackett made an able, though brief, opening argument for the prosecution.

The speaking of the attorneys on the other side was lengthy and irrelevant. In it the killing was scarcely ever alluded to. Old worn-out fabulous stories about "Mormon" atrocities were dwelt upon, and the alleged vagaries of Joseph Smith and Brigham Young were held up to the jury, for the plain purpose of prejudicing them and bringing about a verdict at variance with the facts. Rudger was unsparingly berated. His action in coming from Utah to Georgia as a witness in the case was characterized as an exhibition of unmitigated assurance. It was insinuated that he doubtless expected to obtain his fees and mileage and thus deplete the county treasury, when he might consider himself fortunate should he succeed in getting away from Dalton alive. This abuse intermingled with covert threats was permitted to go unrebuked by the Court.

Colonel Moore made an elaborate and clear argument for the prosecution, and the concluding one was made by General Hackett.

The court delivered the charge. It was of such a character that the jury could not very well find a verdict of guilty and be in accord with it. The honorable judge appeared to make it a point to furnish a plausible excuse for them to acquit the defendant.

At the end of three days—the time occupied by the proceedings thus far—the jury retired.

While they were absent and presumedly deliberating, a curious incident occurred. The sheriff came into court dragging with him a negro, whose eyes were rolling wildly in his head, his grotesque contortions giving every indication of his being in a state of mortal terror.

He was charged with stealing a gallon of whisky. A jury was empanelled on the spot and he was forthwith tried and found guilty. He plead abjectly for mercy, on the ground that he had a large family and was extremely poor. The judge paid no attention to his pleadings, but arose, gravely and severely commented upon the stealing that was going on in Dalton, which must be put down. He elaborated upon the heinous character of the negro's offense, and sentenced him to one year in the chain gang. The severity of the strictures passed by the judge upon the petty crime of this poor wretch were at such variance with his mildness of demeanor in regard to a brutal and inhuman murder, that the incident placed him in an extremely unenviable light.

Finally the jury in the Standing case returned into court with a verdict of "not guilty." The announcement of this result was greeted with a demonstration among the spectators, favorable to the accused. It also greatly increased the popular feeling against Rudger.

There being no probability of obtaining a verdict against either of the other accused either for murder or manslaughter, Bradley and Blair were each tried under the count of the indictment charging them with riot. The result was the same as in the first case—both were acquitted.

The current of popular animous against Rudger, after the trials were concluded, increased in intensity, and considering it unsafe to remain any longer than necessary, he resolved to leave for home as soon a practicable. This determination was confirmed on the evening of the day of the last trial. A gentleman came to him and said: "I hope you will excuse me, Mr. Clawson, being an entire stranger, for addressing you. I am, however, desirous for your safety. A scheme has been developed to have you arrested on a charge of perjury and placed in prison. I would advise you to get away as soon as possible."

He thanked the stranger. He was up and about next morning bright and early, and with the first train he was being whirled toward his home in the West, where he arrived in safety in a few days.

Thus ends the story of one of the most inhuman and inexcusable murders on the record of the State of Georgia. The character of the deed could scarcely be exceeded in point of cowardice, the victim being unarmed, defenseless and completely in the power of his assassins. The fact that the perpetrators were allowed to go unwhipped of justice, notwithstanding that their guilt was clearly proved, is a black stain upon the escutcheon of the State in which the tragedy occurred.

Joseph Standing was twenty-six years of age, of medium height and somewhat stout build, his weight being probably one hundred and sixty pounds. His hair was light and complexion fair. He was noted for his agreeable manners, which were so engaging that he made friends everywhere. He had fair ability as a public speaker, and was an indefatigable minister of the Gospel.

At the time his life was taken he had already served sixteen months of a second mission to the Southern States, and had been for some time in daily expectation of being notified of an honorable release to return home. He had been indulging in gleeful anticipations of meeting soon

with valued friends and loved ones, but these were
cruelly cut short of realization by the bullet of
the cowardly assassin.

In Salt Lake cemetery where the remains ot
the young martyr were interred, there stands
over the tomb a handsome monument, of Italian
marble, with data pertaining to the tragedy in-
scribed upon it. These, however, are all elaborated in this sketch. Upon that memento—which
was erected by subscriptions of members of the
Young Men's Improvement Associations of the
Salt Lake Stake of Zion and others—appears the
following lines from the brilliant pen of Orson
F. Whitney:

Beneath this stone, by friendship's hand, is lain
The martyred form of one, untimely slain ;
A Servant of the Lord, whose works revealed
The love of Truth for which his doom was sealed.

Where foes beset—when but a single friend
Stood true, nor shunned his comrade's cruel end—
Deep in the shades of ill-starred Georgia's wood,
Fair freedom's soil was crimsoned with his blood.

Our brother rests beneath his native sod,
His murderers are in the hands of God.
Weep, weep for them, not him whose silent dust
Here waits the resurrection of the just.

APPENDIX.

CHAPTER I.

The Utah Penitentiary, Enclosure and Buildings.

OWING to the large number of well known, good and true men who have suffered, are suffering and others who are likely to suffer incarceration in the Utah Penitentiary, for conscience sake, that institution has a peculiar interest to the community of Latter-day Saints. Its character may also be a matter of concern to other people as well. In future times it will doubtless occupy a more or less conspicuous niche in the history of this Territory and of the Church. On this account a succint description of the prison is appended, together with a concise statement in relation to the brethren who have been confined there up to date of publication—for polygamy and unlawful cohabitation under the cruel and rigorous regime prescribed by the Edmund's law of 1882, carried out and applied with merciless rigor by those in whose hands its administration has rested.

The fact that one of the chief actors in the story of the Georgia tragedy is an inmate of the penitentiary, and that the details of the narrative were there obtained from him by the author, are additional reasons for the penning of this appendix, as a fitting and probably more or less useful conclusion to this volume.

The Utah Penitentiary occupies a somewhat elevated site, a few miles south by east of Salt Lake City. It fronts westward, and along that line are the residence and office of the Warden, the culinary department, the shops and stables. Those are all ranged along the exterior of the prison proper, the entrance to which is on the same side.

The outer aspect of the place is of small interest compared with that of its interior, and it is, therefore, only the latter that we need to describe. Perhaps this can best be done by taking the reader into and through it on an imaginary visit.

We first go through the outer gateway into a court formed on the west by the entrance through which we have just passed; on the north by the Warden's house; on the south by a storehouse and private cell; and on the east by the wall of the enclosure within which the convicts are confined. In that part of the wall is the entrance, which constitutes the only opening in it. Two large heavy gates are set in the wall. The first is constructed of stout timbers, which cross each other diagonally. The second is the heavier, also of wood, but built solid. When the turnkey lets us through the first, which is not more than four feet from the other, he at once closes it, and we remain within the narrow space between until, by an ingenious attachment, he opens the second. We then step within the enclosure and the ponderous gate closes behind us.

We are then in a large open yard, one acre in extent. It is not exactly square, being somewhat longer from east to west, than from north to south. It is surrounded by an unbroken wall twenty feet in height and four feet thick. It has a foundation of sandstone, the rest of the material being adobies. With the exception of the tips of some of the highest of the adjacent mountains, which can be seen from one or two points of the yard, it effectively shuts out the surrounding scenery from the view of the hapless inmate, who thus has but small facility for relieving the eye, and consequently the mind, by gazing upon the beauties of nature.

Around the entire extent of the wall's exterior is a platform, the floor of which is about three

6

feet from the top. Along this the outside guards on duty patrol—each carrying a rifle—when they are not in the turrets, which are a species of sentry-box, with windows so placed as to enable the watcher to look outward to every point of the compass. They are two in number, one on the north-east corner and the other on the south-west corner. The other two corners are so constructed that one can be placed on each when desirable. Up to the present two have been deemed sufficient.

All the buildings within the enclosure are constructed of wood. With the exception of the eating room and bath house, they are built of pine planks—mostly two inches thick by eight inches wide. The walls are formed by laying those boards flat, one upon the other and fastening them together with large iron spikes, the four corners being jointed. The ceiling is made similarly, the edges of the plank forming the surface. The floor is constructed after the same pattern as the ceiling, the entire structure, both on the exterior and on the inside, having a decidedly ribby aspect. The whole is covered by an ordinary shingle roof.

Near the north-west corner stands an insignificant and squatty structure, as will be judged by its interior dimensions, its width being about ten and its length twelve feet. The height is proportionate. Inside is a strong iron cage, which monopolizes most of the space, as it is about seven feet long and six wide, the height being probably six feet six inches. This sad-looking edifice is used for a variety of purposes. The meagre facilities of this whole institution renders this extensive utilization absolutely necessary. Occasionally it does duty as a hospital for the sick, the number of patients being necessarily limited to one, and of attendants the same.

It has occasionally also been utilized as a place of solitary confinement for refractory convicts, who have gone beyond the bounds prescribed by rules of the prison.

Another capacity in which it has figured has been that of an insane asylum on a small scale, that being the place where the notorious Mike Sullivan has spent a good many lonely hours, in order that he might be prevented from doing bodily harm to his fellow convicts, being a lunatic of the desperate and dangerous type. A law passed by the late Legislature provides for the placing of insane convicts in the Territorial Lunatic Asylum, so that the prison will in future be happily free from that class of unfortunates.

Near the other corner—the south-west—to the right of the entrance to the yard, is another structure of the same character. Indeed it is almost the counterpart of the one just described, including the iron-cage interior attachment. That is the cell in which Fred. Hopt, the oft-convicted murderer of John F. Turner, passes his hours of solitary confinement, pending the final disposal of the case and himself. His only relief from this forbidding loneliness is obtained by him when he paces the few yards of open space in the yard, in the immediate vicinity of his lodging house.

Between, and a short distance from the two structures already described, are two others. So far as their appearance is concerned they are totally unworthy of notice. In some respects, however, they occupy a prominent position in this prison. The use to which they are put renders them objects of some curiosity to people who might merely visit the penitentiary, while to some of the convicts they are peculiarly repulsive. They are each about five feet six inches long, by two feet six inches wide, inside measurement, and have but a solitary opening, in the shape of a door about twenty inches wide and three and a half feet long. These pigmy structures are known by the suggestive title of "sweat boxes." This was perhaps originally designed for summer application, or maybe they were erected during the heated term, and the first inmates very likely were incarcerated while the thermometer in the ordinary shade was in the nineties, and in their interior climbed considerably higher. While there is a striking adaptability about the title under such warm conditions, in winter they might, with equal propriety, be denominated the "refrigerators." These little dens are used as places of solitary confinement for the more contumacious offenders against the discipline of the prison. The victim who is consigned to that species of punishment, even for a limited period, is greatly to be pitied. There are few who endure it long, being generally willing to come to terms, and place themselves on their good behavior on short notice.

Facing the gate in a line are the two most pretentious buildings of the interior. They are the bunk-houses or cells, where the prisoners are locked up at nights. The first incorporates bunk-houses, Numbers One and Two, the former being the first reached as we advance eastward. Attached to its front is a small room used as a guard house, for the use of the officers on duty inside the inclosure.

The dimensions of the interior are : thirty feet long by twenty feet wide, the height from floor to ceiling being twelve feet. The visitor is instantly impressed with the comfortless appearance of the room, and the rigid economy that has been used in the utilization of a limited space. The manner in which the sleeping acommodations are arranged reminds one forcibly of the passenger steerage of a large ship. The sleeping bunks extend entirely around three walls, that which contains the entrance being the only one exempt from those peculiar sleepers. They are in three tiers, being one over another, the space between being about three feet. Each bunk is six feet six inches long, by four feet six inches wide, and parallel with the wall lengthwise. The number of bunks in Number One is thirty-two, and as each is intended for two inmates, there is sleeping accommodation in that particular cell for sixty-four convicts, and it has been of late generally almost if not quite full.

Around the room, in front of the lower tier of bunks, is a rough board, placed on uprights which does duty as a seat.

Inserted in the upper part of the walls—almost close up to the ceiling—are four windows, each about two feet square. These windows are protected on the outside by strong iron bars. As they are set back, beyond the upper bunks, the light from them is necessarily refracted, and is consequently largely diminished by the time it reaches the middle of the room; the general aspect is, to say the least, somewhat sombre. This effect suffers no diminution by the hanging up in front of some of the bunks, upon strings stretched from post to post, of various articles of underwear, some of them by no means refreshingly new.

Near the centre of the ceiling there is a square aperture, crossed liberally with flat iron bars. This contrivance, connected with a suitable opening in the roof, serves the purpose of a ventilator, a convenience that, it is scarcely requisite to state, is highly necessary.

There is but one entrance to the cell—a strong door made of iron bars, crossing each other at intervals of four inches, and fastened together with rivets, or, considering their size, they might as appropriately be called bolts. None of the men convicted of polygamy or unlawful cohabitation have thus far been confined in Number One.

Bunk house Number Two is in the same building, and is in general features similar to that just described. It is considerably smaller, however, being twenty by twenty feet, and has only two, in place of three, tiers of bunks; consequently its sleeping accommodations are but one-half that of the other. They have of late been fully utilized. Quite a sprinkling of the brethren have been quartered in that compartment for some time.

Number Three is detached from the other bunk houses, being situated a few feet further eastward. It is a recent addition to the premises, having been erected in the summer of 1885. It is similar to the others. It is twenty-six feet long and twenty feet wide. There are, as in Number One, three tiers of bunks, of which there are twenty-six, the room thus affording sleeping conveniences for fifty-two convicts. There are five small windows, protected by iron gratings, of the same size as those heretofore described. Thus far the sole occupants—varying from forty to fifty in number—have been men convicted of unlawful cohabitation, and prisoners who are employed in various capacities on the outside of the penitentiary proper. They are called "trusties," the title being derived from the fact that their occupations give them opportunities to escape, which it is not presumed they will take advantage of, besides their being necessarily trusted in other respects.

In warm weather these cells are infested with vermin in the shape of bed bugs. The interstices between the planks give them ample breeding facilities, which they do not hesitate to take advantage of. The consequence is, that they make incursions in "shoals and nations," subjecting the hapless convicts to annoyance that falls but little, if anything, short of torture. Different remedies have been employed upon this plague of the prison, but thus far they have only mitigated the evil without approaching its abatement.

Before giving a description of what is, somewhat inaptly, called the dining hall, it may be well to state that immediately west of it is a small guard house, used as a sleeping apartment by the guards detailed for inside duty. The long, low building in which the eating room is situated, runs from west to east, parallel with the bunk houses, a short lane or street, about twenty-two feet wide, being thus formed.

The word dining-hall is generally associated with ideas of comfort, with concomitant surroundings of an attractive character. This is why the title, as applied to this apartment, may be justly considered a misnomer. Its conveniences are, to say the least, of a most primitive description, and even at that are the reverse of profuse. Two conditions have contributed to make it much less repulsive to us than it was formerly. The first is a very decided improvement made some time since by Mr. G. N. Dow, the Warden—a very humane gentleman by the way—in the shape of a couple of large skylights, which give the place an air of comparative cheerfulness by letting in the sunlight of heaven. The second is familiarity, which soon begins to dispel the more gloomy aspect of the surroundings of a person who philosophically determines to "make the best of a bad job."

The feeling of repulsion with which we were seized on our first entrance to the room is vividly remembered. The pleasure of our debut, as a partaker of the frugal repast provided by "Uncle Sam," was not increased by the first sounds we heard from the interior of the dining hall. As Andrew Smith and ourself first entered the prison, out of that particular room, where a large number of convicts were crowded together, came "bow-wows," whoops, shouts and yells of "hang him."

These threatening utterances were directed against my companion, who, in his capacity of police officer, appeared to have gained the ill-will of some of the rougher prisoners.

Inappropriate as it may be, we will adhere to the title by which the room is known. It is fifty-four feet long by nineteen wide. The material used in its construction is simply inch weather boarding, nailed to a studding frame, the timbers being set at unusually wide distances apart. The height to the square is about seven feet six inches. There is no ceiling, the bare shingles being the only obstacle between the inmates and the heavenly expanse. The cross braces by which the frame of the roof is stayed are generally adorned with shirts, stockings, and articles of underwear generally, making the place smack somewhat of "Rag Fair," London. Occasionally from the same raised position a couple of "exalted soles"—hob-nailed attachments to a dilapidated pair of boots—look grimly down from whence they are suspended.

No part of the interior is plastered, there being but an inch board to the weather. Here and there the thin walls are plastered over with gaudy pictures clipped from periodicals of the day, according to the taste or fancy of the convict whose seat happens to be near the particular spot thus decorated. For convenience' sake, little narrow shelves have been nailed to the wall, and on these are old fruit cans, the tin pint cup with which each convict is furnished, and other articles.

Against the wall, and skirting the entire room, at the height of an ordinary table, is a rough deal board, two feet wide. This serves for a table. Each convict fortunate enough to secure a place at this board is allotted a space of twenty-two inches in width, giving barely enough elbow room at meal times. The seating convenience at this table consists of a rough plank, two inches thick and eight inches wide, supported, a short distance outward from the side-table, upon uprights consisting of pieces of the same material. The seating space allotted to each is of the same length as and parallel with the tabular apportionment.

As over one hundred men sit down at each meal, the room is, as may well be imagined, at such times always crowded. Consequently the side-tables are far from being sufficient, and there are four or five large tables besides, ranged down the centre of the room. But they are not so popular with the convicts as the seats along the wall, owing to the latter perhaps being slightly more retired, if such a term could be appropriately used in connection with so great a crowd.

Besides the two sky-lights lately added, the room is lighted by means of nine windows, each of which has nine squares of glass, measuring eight by ten inches.

Upon the east end of the dining hall, being a continuation of the same building, are the bath-room and wash-house, where the convicts are required to perform their ablutions. These apartments are among the most convenient and attractive of any in the prison, being neatly painted. They are kept in a condition of scrupulous cleanliness by Robert Taylor, familiar-ly called " Bob," the man in charge.

CHAPTER II.

Officers.—Prison Fare.—Discipline.'

THE officers of the prison consist of the Warden, Turnkey, and eight Guards. The will of the first named official is supreme under the law and the United States Marshal, the supervisory oversight of the penitentiary devolving upon the latter.

The duty of the Turnkey is to have personal supervision of the ingress to and egress from the prison of all persons, and to look after other matters unnecessary to notice in this description. Being the next official in rank to the Warden, he usually has entire charge whenever that officer happens to be absent. In case of the absence of the Turnkey one of the guards is detailed to attend to the duties of his office.

The labors of the guards are so arranged that each one is alternately six hours on and off duty. Two are constantly, night and day, on the walls, being stationed in the sentry-boxes or turrets, or patroling to and fro upon the platform, rifle in hand. Their position enables them to have a full view of the yard, so that, in case of a violent outbreak or attempted escape, they can, in an emergency, fire upon the offenders.

Two are always in the yard to attend to all mat-. ters within the prison proper. Formerly those detailed for interior duty carried fire-arms; this practice has been discontinued, as it was discovered to be attended by no small degree of danger. Several plots, which were nipped in the bud, were found to include an intention to disarm the guards, who would, in case the schemes had carried, have been at the mercy of the conspiring convicts.

One or other of the officers on duty in the interior are required to make the round of the yard every fifteen minutes during the night, to see that all is right and everything secure. To neglect this duty renders the offender liable to discharge. It is next to impossible for it to be shirked or even omitted, from any cause, without its being detected. In the guard-room there is a "regulator" with a dial face. The guard on duty must touch a point of this contrivance with his finger every fifteen minutes. By this means a paper ribbon in the interior of the "regulator" is pricked. There is a similar instrument in each of the turrets, so that the guards on the wall are subject to the same mechanical surveillance. Each man is, therefore, under the necessity of being sleeplessly at his post. The regulators are examined every morning by the Warden.

The safety of the prison is further maintained by rendering any further dereliction otherwise discoverable by the guards, those inside and those upon the wall being checks on each other. When the man in the interior first starts out upon each of his frequent night patrols, he signals with his lantern to both of those upon the wall, and they respond to him by elevating two lamps suspended by wires from the turrets down the wall to within a few feet of the ground. It is a part of the duty of each guard to report any serious instance of neglect on the part of any of the others.

For almost every species of general operation in the yard, signals are given by the ringing of bells by the guard stationed on the south-west corner of the wall.

From a quarter past five to half-past six in the evening, according to the season of the year, earlier in winter and later in summer, three bells are rung for the convicts to prepare to enter the bunk houses. Those belonging to Number One are attended to first. They form in line, from the door outward, and as soon as the word is given they pass in, one at a time, and are counted by the guards as they enter, to make sure that none are missing. Then Number Two and Three follow in respective order.

As soon as the prisoners are within, the heavy iron door is closed and the ponderous bars are adjusted.

The convicts spend the time intervening between the locking-up hour and the hour for retiring as best they may. It is not the intention to give, in these details, a pen-picture of the generality of these evening proceedings. We will probably do so on a future occasion.

The " trusties," to the number of fourteen, who are lodged in Number Three, to which we belonged, are admitted subsequent to the locking-up of the ordinary convicts, as their labors continue for some time after the regular hour for entering the cells.

Precisely at nine o'clock the guard appears at the door, upon which he delivers a number of raps, to attract attention. He then gives the word for all to " turn in." According to the rule all conversation must cease, and the prisoners retire for the night.

At a quarter past five in the morning those trusties employed in the cooking department are awakened by the guard, and fifteen minutes afterward they are allowed to pass out to begin the labors of the day. Shortly before seven the clanking of the bars and the grating sound of the iron door as it swings open are again heard. All are then required to arise, dress, make up their beds, and go out to the wash-house, and perform their morning ablutions.

The floor of each bunk house is swept every

7

morning, each man taking his turn in the performance of this duty. It is carefully scrubbed twice a week, five men being detailed for that purpose, alternating so that the work is equally divided among the prisoners.

In dry weather five men are appointed daily to perform police duty in the yard, which is simply to clean up and keep the premises in order.

Eight men are detailed to act as waiters. They have the general oversight of the dining hall, keeping it clean, serving meals, etc.

At eight o'clock each morning one bell is rung. This is the signal for the waiters to go to the gate and bring in the food; also for convicts to place their tin pint cups to receive their ration of coffee, on their allotted places at the tables. All are then required to clear out of the room.

The morning meal consists of coffee without sugar or milk, bread, meat, and a couple of melancholy potatoes to each man. The sadness of the tubers is caused by their being cooked the night previous. Every other day the meat portion of the programme is omitted, being substituted by a mysterious compound called hash. The meat and coffee are brought to the dining hall in huge vessels made of galvanized iron, and the bread, cut in slices, in ordinary brown wicker bushel baskets. The only table utensils given for the use of the convicts are a tin pint cup, an iron spoon, and a common tin plate to each. Knives and forks are not allowed, owing to the danger of having such utensils around the place.

For dinner, which is served between twelve and one o'clock, bread, meat and potatoes compose the bill of fare one day, followed every alternate day by an unsubstantial article of soup, to which a couple of slices of bread constitute the solitary accompaniment.

The evening meal, which is disposed of shortly before five o'clock, is " without shadow of turning," its components being bread and a tin cupful of sugarless and milkless tea.

The manner of entering the dining hall for meals is worth noting. At a given signal the convicts form into two lines, extending eastward from the door, where the guard stands for the purpose of enforcing order. The signal is then given to file in, and the prisoners enter two abreast, and take their places at the tables.

Each prisoner must perform complete bodily ablutions, by means of the bath, once a week in summer, and once in two weeks in winter.

The convicts generally wash their own clothing in the yard. A few, however, send their washing to town, the packages being searched both in going and returning, to prevent breaches of the rules in relation to correspondence with persons on the outside, etc.

The hair of each convict is clipped close to the scalp once a month, and the face is shaved clean once a week.

All correspondence, outgoing and incoming, is examined by the Warden. If, in his judgment, any communication contains aught objectionable, it is not permitted to go out. Letters, books, and periodicals, excepting local newspapers, can be received at any time The latter are not admitted to the prison. Ordinarily convicts are permitted to write to friends on the outside twice a month, but oftener, by special permission, should some unusual emergency demand.

The friends of convicts are allowed to see them —providing they first obtain a pass from the U. S. Marshal—on the first Thursday of each month. Those having passes are not allowed to enter the prison proper, but are conducted to an apartment used as a dining room by the guards. The officer on the west wall, after the bell has been rung once, calls out the name of the convict

on the permit. The visited prisoner is let out
at the gate, and goes to the room where the
visitors are in waiting. He sits on one side of a
long table and they on the other, and the conversation must be conducted in a tone sufficiently
loud to be heard by a guard, who is stationed at
the end of the table for the purpose of seeing
that no objectionable communication passes between the parties. The interview terminates at
the end of thirty minutes, when the convict re-
enters the yard, and the visitors take their leave.

Visitors are frequently allowed to stand upon
the platform which runs parallel with the
outside of the wall, and from that elevated
position obtain a view of the yard and buildings.
They are not permitted, however, to give any
sign of recognition to the prisoners. Neither are
the latter allowed to recognize their friends, but
the parties may gaze at each other. The position
is frequently, to say the least, exceedingly painful
on both sides.

Religious services are held every Sunday after-
noon. They are conducted by the clergymen of
the different sects—excepting those of the Roman
Catholic Church—alternately, the Episcopalians
officiating twice during the particular months in
which there happens to be five Sabbath days.

The turn of the Latter-day Saints comes on the first Sunday of each month.

Three bells are always a signal to the prisoners. When that is heard they are on the alert to hear some general order, which is occasionally for all to go up to the north-east corner of the yard. This signifies that some official or other more or less distinguished visitor is about to enter.

A wire is stretched from north to south, about twelve paces east of the west wall. It is called the "dead line." A prisoner is not allowed to cross it to the westward except for special purposes. Before he does so he must signal the guard on the wall by raising one hand. If he receives the usual response he can proceed. If not, he is not permitted to cross, or does so at his peril.

Each convict is clothed in the usual zebraic costume common in United States prisons generally.

More minute details, involving the whole of the discipline, might be given, but it appears to be unnecessary.

Breaches of the rules are punishable in various ways. The penalties are to some degree defined by statute, but in a general way they are within the discretion of the Warden, under the U. S. Marshal.

CHAPTER III.

Those who have been Incarcerated for conscience' sake.—
Their Offenses, Pleas, and Penalties.—Brief Biographical
Notes and Personal References.

RUDGER CLAWSON ; plea, not guilty ; sentenced November 3rd, 1884, by Judge Zane, on conviction for polygamy, to imprisonment for three years and six months and to pay a fine of $500; unlawful cohabitation, six months and $300, being four years and $800 in all. The case was appealed to the Supreme Court of the Territory, which sustained the judgment of the lower court. He was born in Salt Lake City, March 12th, 1857, and has been in the Church from childhood, his parents being connected with it at the time of his birth.

JOSEPH H. EVANS; plea, not guilty; polygamy and unlawful cohabitation; sentenced, by Judge Zane, November 8th, 1884; three years and six months, and a fine of $500. He was born at Llanelly, Carmarthenshire, Wales, August 12th, 1820; joined the Church in July, 1850, and came to Utah in 1854. His height is about five feet nine inches. He is of portly build, and has a

Celtic face. He is outspoken, almost to bluntness, and possesses a large degree of religious zeal. He is a blacksmith and has resided in Salt Lake City nearly the whole time he has been in Utah.

PARLEY P. PRATT; unlawful cohabitation; plea of guilty; sentenced by Judge Zane, May 2nd, 1885; term, six months; fine, $300. He was born at Kirtland, Ohio, March 25th, 1837, and is the eldest son of the late Apostle Parley P. Pratt. He has been with the Church from his birth to the present, and in his childhood passed through the stirring scenes of its early history. He came to Utah in 1848, and has been on several missions abroad. He has brown hair and a medium complexion. His head is small, and face and features round. His height is six feet, and build slender.

ANGUS M. CANNON; unlawful cohabitation; plea of not guilty; sentenced May 9th, 1885, by Judge Zane; term, six months; fine, $300 and costs. The case was appealed to the Supreme Court of the Territory, and taken on a writ of error to the Supreme Court of the U. S., both of which tribunals sustained the lower courts. Pending the final adjudication by the U. S.

Supreme Court the defendant remained in jail about two months over the term of sentence, the chief object being to obtain an authoritative definition of the legal scope of the term "unlawful cohabitation." On Monday, May 10th, 1886, three cases of unlawful cohabitation against Lorenzo Snow were disposed of by the U. S. Supreme Court, to which they had been appealed. The court decided it had no jurisdiction. To show consistency it reconsidered its mandate in Brother Cannon's appeal and dismissed that case also. The court could not well continue the position of having jurisdiction in the one case and not in the others, all of them being of the same class. Brother Cannon was born in Liverpool, England, May 17th, 1834. His parents having joined the Church under the administration of President John Taylor in 1840, the family left England for Nauvoo in 1842. His mother died during the voyage across the Atlantic. Brother Angus was baptized in the Mississippi River, near Nauvoo, in the fall of 1844. He was driven out of that place with the body of the Saints. After enduring many hardships, he came to Utah in 1849. He was engaged in various occupations, and spent some time in founding settlements and building up southern Utah. In 1852 he engaged in the printing business, in the *Deseret News* office, and in 1854 went on a mission to the Eastern States with Apostle John Taylor, returning home in 1858. He went to the Utah "Dixie," and with Erastus Snow and Jacob Gates located the city of St. George, of which he was Mayor for four years. He came back to Salt Lake, and in 1868 entered the *Deseret News* office as its business manager, a position he occupied six years, afterwards engaging in the business of dealing in wagons and machinery. In the spring of 1876 he was appointed President of Salt Lake Stake, his present ecclesiastical position. He was Recorder for Salt Lake County a number of years. He is over medium height and proportionate build; complexion dark. His face is round and somewhat full.

AMOS MILTON MUSSER; unlawful cohabitation; plea of not guilty; sentenced May 9th, 1885; term, six months; fine, $300 and costs. Appealed to the Territorial Supreme Court, which sustained the judgment of the court below. He was born in Donegal Township, Lancaster County, Pa. His father died when he was little more than an infant, and a few years afterwards his mother and eldest sister joined the Church. The family removed to Nauvoo, Illinois, in 1846, and were, the same year, driven out by mob violence at the time of the general expulsion of the Saints. Brother Musser joined the Church, by baptism, in 1851, in Iowa, and came to Utah the same year. He was sent on a mission in 1852 to Hindostan, East Indies, and was absent five years. While so engaged he learned to speak the Hindostanee language with a fair degree of fluency, and to read and write it readily in the Arabic characters. He was employed for nineteen years under Presidents B. Young, D. H. Wells, Geo. A. Smith, and Bishop Hunter, as a Traveling Bishop and Agent. He filled a brief mission to the States in 1876.

JAMES C. WATSON; unlawful cohabitation; plea of guilty; sentenced May 9th, 1885, by Judge Zane; term, six months; fine, $300. He was born at Newart Hill, Lanarkshire, Scotland, September 4th, 1844, his father being then in the Church. His mother was not then a member, and insisted that James should be christened in the Presbyterian Church. She accordingly took him there and that ordinance was attended to. On her way home she declared that the Lord gave her a testimony of the truth of the Gospel as revealed through Joseph Smith, and she was consequently baptized a short time afterwards. James was baptized when eight years old, and came with the family to America in 1848; remained in St. Louis till 1850, when he came to Salt Lake City, where he has resided ever since. He is large and portly, being in height five feet eleven inches, and turns the scale at two hundred and thirty pounds. He has fair complexion and blue eyes, and is noted for the hearty cordiality of his manners, being the embodiment of good nature.

WILLIAM FOTHERINGHAM; unlawful cohabitation; plea of not guilty; sentenced May 20th, 1885, by Judge Boreman; term, three months; fine, $300. He was born at Clackmannan, Clackmannanshire, Scotland, April 5th, 1826; joined the Church in 1847; came to America in 1848, and stayed in the States till 1850, when he came to Utah. Performed a mission to the East Indies and another to the Cape of Good Hope, South Africa. He is the senior member of the High Council of Beaver Stake, Agent for the Presiding Bishop, and has been Superintendent of Sunday Schools in that part of the Territory from the beginning of their organization. He was Clerk of Beaver County seventeen years; Mayor of Beaver City two years; Justice of the Peace four years; and has represented the counties of Beaver, Iron and Piute, in the Council of the Territorial Legislature. When the "move" south occurred in anticipation of the entry of Albert Sidney Johnston's army, Elder Fotheringham was one of a number of men detailed to lay Salt Lake City in ashes, should such a recourse be deemed necessary.

FRANCIS A. BROWN; unlawful cohabitation; plea of not guilty; sentenced July 11th, 1885, by Judge Powers; term, six months; fine, $300. The defendant made a speech in court in which he asserted that he would rather have his head severed from his body than prove recreant to his religious obligations, which, he held, were in-volved in the case. He was born in New York State, November 14th, 1822. He joined the Church and went to Nauvoo, Illinois, in 1844, and came to Utah in 1856. He settled in Ogden, of which town he has been a resident ever since. He is a little over medium height, has a strong, honest face, characteristic of his nature, which is ruggedly resolute. He performed a mission to Holland.

MORONI BROWN; unlawful cohabitation; plea of not guilty; sentenced July 11th, 1885, by Judge Powers; term, six months; fine, $300. He stated in court that he did not propose to renounce his religious principles to conform to any law. He was born in Adam's County, Illinois, September 25th, 1840, his parents being then connected with the Church; shortly afterwards the family removed to Nauvoo; were driven out at the time of the expulsion, and came to Utah in 1851. His father purchased a large tract of land, including the site on which Ogden now stands, from the original settler, he being the founder of that city. Moroni is over the over the average height, heavily built; his hair and complexion are dark. He filled a mission to Europe.

JOB PINGREE; unlawful cohabitation; plea of not guilty; sentenced July 13th, 1885, by Judge Powers; term, five months; fine, $300 and costs. His case was one in which the court exhibited the most heartless cruelty, combined with canting hypocrisy, as the author proposes, at some future time, to show. He was born in Gloucestershire, England, November 21st, 1837; came to Utah in 1857, and settled in Ogden, where he has resided ever since. He is tall, slender, and active. His head and features are small, and complexion medium. He is intensely practical, and has taken a prominent part in the public affairs of the community among whom he lives.

JOHN LANG; unlawful cohabitation; plea of guilty; sentenced September 29th, 1885, by Judge Boreman; term, three months; fine, $200. He was born in Devonshire, England, March 15th, 1831. He joined the Church by baptism in 1840, and came to Utah in 1855. He is a farmer, and resided in Salt Lake City six years; spent ten years on the southern frontier, and finally settled in Beaver—his present place of residence—in 1871. He is a man of exceptional simplicity and honesty of character.

H. B. CLAWSON, Bishop of the Twelfth Ward, Salt Lake City; unlawful cohabitation; plea of guilty; sentenced September 29th, 1885, by Judge Zane; term, six months; fine, $300 and costs. He was born in Utica, N. Y., November 7th, 1826; was baptized in childhood, and removed in early times to Nauvoo, with his mother and other relatives. Was driven from that place at the time of the expulsion of the Saints, and came to Utah in 1848.

EDWARD BRAIN; unlawful cohabitation; plea of not guilty; sentenced October 2nd, 1885, by Judge Zane; term, six months; fine, $300 and costs. He was born at Wick, Gloucestershire, England, August 15th, 1821, and joined the Church in August, 1844, at Bath. He came to Utah in 1852. He is a builder by trade.

CHARLES SEAL; unlawful cohabitation; plea of not guilty; sentenced October 5th, 1885, by Judge Zane; term, six months; fine, $300 and costs. He was born at Qounton, Gloucestershire, England, January 18th, 1834; joined the Church in the winter of 1844, and came to Utah in 1871.

CHARLES L. WHITE; unlawful cohabitation; plea of guilty; sentenced October 6th, 1885, by Judge Zane; term, six months; fine, $300 and costs. The plea of guilty was made by arrangement with the Prosecuting Attorney upon an agreement that a charge of polygamy be withdrawn. His plural wife, Elizabeth Ann Starkey, had been imprisoned in the penitentiary two months and twenty-one days for refusing to answer certain questions propounded by Commissioner McKay, examining magistrate, and the grand jury; the understanding with the prosecution alluded to resulting in her release. C. L. White was born at Forest Green, Gloucestershire, England, June 26th, 1857. He was baptized at the age of eight years, and came to Utah in 1874. He is a resident of Salt Lake City, and follows the trade of brush-maker.

JOHN CONNELLY; unlawful cohabitation; plea of guilty; sentenced October 5th, 1885, by Judge Zane; term, six months; fine, $300 and costs. He was born (of Irish parents) at Berwick-on-Tweed, Scotland, February 12th, 1853. He joined the Church in 1870, and came to Utah in 1871.

DAVID E. DAVIS; unlawful cohabitation; plea of not guilty; sentenced October 5th, 1885, by Judge Zane; term, six months; fine, $300 and costs. He was born at Rhymney, Monmouthshire, England, September, 1841; joined the Church May 30th, 1865; came to Utah November 16th, 1863. He is a resident of Tooele County, and is a farmer, stockraiser, and telegraph operator, having been in the employ· of the Western Union Company several years in the latter capacity. He is short of stature, round faced, and has dark eyes and hair.

8

ISAAC GROO; unlawful cohabitation; plea of guilty; sentenced October 5th, 1885, by Judge Zane; term, six months; fine, $300 and costs. He was born in Sullivan County, N. Y., April 8th, 1827; joined the Church January 1st, 1852, and came to Utah in 1854. He has occupied a number of official positions connected with the municipality of Salt Lake City—notably Supervisor of Streets, agent for the city, Alderman and Councilor. He was also Bishop's Counselor in the Ninth Ward from 1856 to 1877, having occupied that relation to three different Bishops —Seth Taft, John Woolley and Samuel A. Woolley. His hair, eyes, and complexion are dark, his height five feet ten inches, and his build proportionate. He is a man of much over the average intelligence, and has read extensively.

ALFRED BEST; unlawful cohabitation; plea of guilty; sentenced October 5th, 1885, by Judge Zane; term, six months; fine, $300 and costs, He was born in Toddington, Gloucestershire. England, June 19th, 1829; joined the Church in Birmingham, in 1849; came to Utah in 1851. He is a resident of Salt Lake City. He is short of stature and spare build. His eyes and complexion are dark, and his constitution by no means robust. He is a tinner by trade, but retired from that business several years ago.

ANDREW W. COOLEY; unlawful cohabitation; plea of guilty; sentenced October 5th, 1885, by Judge Zane; term, six months; fine, $300 and costs. He was born at Bruce, McComb County, Michigan, May 24th, 1837, and in 1863 came to Utah, where he joined the Church in 1864. He is a large framed man, with medium complexion and blue eyes. He was Bishop of Brighton Ward from 1865 to 1871, when he resigned.

WILLIAM A. ROSSITER; .unlawful cohabitation;. plea of not guilty; sentenced October 10th, 1885, by Judge Zane; term, six months and $300 and costs. A conspicuous feature of the case was the flimsy character of the evidence produced by the prosecutor. Speaking of this feature of it, a prominent lawyer remarked that he saw no use of a "Mormon" making any legal fight; he being convinced that to accuse was to convict. W. A. Rossiter was born in London, England, February 26th, 1843; joined the Church, at Barnsley, in 1860, and started for Utah in 1862. A thrilling incident in his experience occurred at Florence,

Wyoming, the point of outfitting for crossing the plains. He worked for the Church there, conveying the emigrants and their luggage from the landing on the Missouri river to the camp, a distance of about half a mile. He was leaving the landing with his ox-teams and wagon, with a load, when a terrible rain and thunderstorm arose. He stopped a short distance from the camp, and the fifteen people who accompanied him crouched under the wagon considerably terrified. Finding there was no abatement of the storm, Brother Rossiter advised them to take their luggage and seek better shelter. All had gone except a man named Day, another named Henry B. Whittall—formerly assistant editor of the *Millennial Star*—and a young woman and a boy. William was in the act of raising his whip, and was about to say "gee" to the cattle, when he felt a sensation as if he was whirling round like a top, and then he became unconscious. When he partially recovered he found himself lying upon the ground, abount ten feet from where he had been standing, with his head between the wheels, Wben he rose to his feet he staggered about for some time. He was shocked to discover Whittall lying with his head under the wagon quite dead. and Day a short distance away in a dying condition, while the young woman and boy were badly hurt, all having been struck by lightning. His own escape was remarkable. He reached Utah in the fall of the same year, 1862. He successively worked at farming, teaming, and as driver of President Young's carriage. Finally he was employed as his agent, had charge of all his outside business, and is still employed by his estate. While in prison he showed himself to be remarkably kind-hearted and obliging. His height is five feet eight inches, he is of spare build, dark complexion, and has pointed features.

GEORGE ROMNEY; unlawful cohabitation; plea of guilty; sentenced October 10th, 1885, by Judge Zane; term, six months; fine, $300 and costs. He was born at Dalton, Lancashire, England, August 14th, 1831; was baptized when eight years old, and emigrated to Nauvoo, Illinois, in 1841. Was driven from that place at the time the Church was expelled; came to Utah in the fall of 1850. He is a contractor, builder, etc. He is five feet nine and a half inches in height, has auburn hair, and blue eyes. His face is large and carries upon it a reflective expression. He is recognized as the possessor of excellent business ability, which has enabled him to reach a considerable degree of financial prosperity. He is a member of the well-known firm of Taylor, Romney & Armstrong.

JOHN NICHOLSON; unlawful cohabitation. He declined to make any plea, and the court directed that one of not guilty be entered. At the trial, in order to save members of his family from being compelled to testify against him, he took the stand himself, and gave evidence for the prosecution sufficient to insure conviction, making it unnecessary to use any other witness. This was the first case in which this course was taken. He was sentenced by Judge Zane, October 13th, when he addressed the court, and declared his intention to be true to his religion, his family, and his conscientious views of his rights under the Constitution. The term was six months; fine, $300 and costs. He was born at St. Boswells, Roxburghshire, Scotland, July 11th, 1839; joined the Church in Edinburgh, April 8th, 1861, and came to Utah in 1866. His height is five feet eight inches; build, slender; hair, eyes, and complexion dark; profession, journalist.

EMIL OSCAR OLSEN; unlawful cohabitation; plea of guilty; sentenced October 13th, 1885, by

Judge Zane; term, six months; fine, $300 and costs. He was born in Christiania, Norway, September 12th, 1849; joined the Church in 1863, and came to Utah in 1874. He resided in Echo four years, where he was Counselor to Bishop Asper a year and a half. He then removed to Salt Lake City. He is a tailor by trade. He is short and stout; is of fair complexion, and has sandy hair. He is genial and pleasant to a more than ordinary degree.

ANDREW SMITH; unlawful cohabitation; plea of not guilty. He took the stand and testified against himself. Before receiving sentence, which was passed October 13th, 1885, by Judge Zane, he briefly addressed the court, asserting that he did not purpose under any circumstances to renounce his religion. He was born at Linester, Ayrshire, Scotland, February 28th, 1837; joined the Church when he was fourteen years of age, and came to Utah in 1856. On his way here he crossed the plains with a handcart company numbering about six hundred, over eighty of whom perished on the journey. On account of his extraordinary physical strength his cart was so loaded with flour and other people's baggage, that three of those vehicles drawn by him broke

down with their burdens. He has worked in the
Temple quarry, and at various kinds of canyon
work. He had charge of a large force of men
engaged on Bishop Sharp's contract in the building of the U. P. R. R.; was frequently a body
guard to President Brigham Young, and at his
office. He has been on the regular police force of
Salt Lake City fifteen years, besides having previously performed a great deal of special police
duty. His height is five feet ten inches, and he
is of powerful build. His complexion is what is
generally denominated sandy.

AURELIUS MINER; unlawful cohabitation; plea
of not guilty; sentenced October 17th, 1885, by
Judge Zane; term, six months; fine, $300 and
costs. He was born at Woodbury, Lichfield
County, Connecticut, January 11th, 1832, and is
a nephew of the late Apostle Orson Hyde. He
came to Salt Lake City in 1854, arriving September 1st of that year, the object of his trip being
to visit his uncle, by whom he was baptized in
February, 1858. He made the journey across the
plains in the merchant train of Kinney, Green
& Co. Judge Kinney, the then newly appointed
Chief Justice of Utah, George B. Styles, Associate
Justice, and Joseph Holman, U. S. District

Attorney, traveled in the same company. Mr. Miner is a graduate of the State National College of New York, 'and by virtue of his diploma, as Bachelor of Laws, was entitled to practice in that State. He was also member of the bar of Columbus, Ohio, and of the State of Michigan. He was admitted to the bar of the Supreme Court of the U. S. in January, 1883, and up to a recent date was the oldest practitioner in the courts of Utah, having been admitted to the bar in 1854. Shortly after his conviction he was disbarred by Chief Justice Zane, the grounds stated being moral turpitude, alleged to be involved in said conviction, and because he reserved the, right of opinion regarding the constitutionality of any law, and would not promise to obey the Edmunds law in the future. He is of medium height, square build, fair complexion, and has a round face and small features.

WILLIAM D. NEWSOM; polygamy and unlawful cohabitation; plea of not guilty; sentenced October 17th, 1885, by Judge Zane; complete term, three years and six months; fine, $800. He was born in Arklow, County of Wicklow, Ireland, February 21st, 1836. He was baptized in September, 1862, while engaged as a steamboat engineer, on Alago Bay, South Africa, and came to Utah in 1865. He is short and square, has light complexion, and prominent features.

LUCY DEVEREUX, his plural wife, was imprisoned six weeks, with her infant child, in the penitentiary, for declining to answer Commissioner McKay and the grand jury certain questions, one of which was: "Who is the father of your child?"

ROBERT H. SWAIN; unlawful cohabitation; plea of guilty; sentenced November 2nd, 1885, by Judge Zane; term, six months; fine, $300 and costs. He was born March 19th, 1836, in the County of Kent, England. He was baptized in 1854, in Dover, where he was at the time employed as a policeman. He came to Utah in 1865. He is six feet two inches tall, and weighs one hundred and eighty pounds. He has fair complexion, blue eyes, and long features.

FRED. H. HANSEN; unlawful cohabitation; plea of not guilty; sentenced November 5th, 1885, by Judge Zane; term, six months; fine, $300 and costs. He was born at Lolland, Denmark, April 13th, 1845. He was baptized in 1868, and came to Utah in 1878. He is short and square, and has a round or broad face. His complexion is fair.

THOMAS PORCHER; unlawful cohabitation; plea of not guilty; sentenced November 21st, 1885, by Judge Zane; term,. six months; fine, $300 and costs. He was born in Cambridge, England, December 20th, 1839, his parents being then in the Church. He came to Utah in 1861. He was formerly a printer, but is now a tinner and plumber. He is somewhat short of stature, and unusually round in form and feature.

JOHN W. KEDDINGTON; unlawful cohabitation; plea of guilty; sentenced, by Judge Zane, November 21st, 1885; term, six months; fine, $300 and costs. He was born in Leeds, Yorkshire, England, May 15th, 1850; came to Utah in 1853, having consequently been reared in the Church. His principal employment is that of teamster. He is also a musician, and has played the cornet in the orchestra of the Salt Lake Theatre for four years. His height is six feet two inches, and his build is slender.

HENRY GALE; unlawful cohabitation; plea of guilty; sentenced, by Judge Boreman, December

17th, 1885; term, six months and $300. He was born in Box, Wiltshire, England, October 18th, 1818, and went to Australia in 1839, where he joined the Church in 1843. He emigrated to San Bernardino, California, in 1853, and came to Utah in 1857. He settled in Beaver, and has resided there ever since. At the time of sentence he was a confirmed invalid, being unable to dress or undress without aid, being disabled by chronic rheumatism. He was also afflicted with a severe rupture; had only partial control over some of the common functions of the body, and was almost toothless. Comment upon the bar-•barity of incarcerating him is unnecessary. When asked by the court if he had anything to say, he declared that he would not renounce his religion on any condition.

CULBERT KING, Bishop of Marion Ward, Garfield County; unlawful cohabitation; plea of guilty; sentenced December 22nd, 1885, by Judge Boreman; term, six months; fine, $300 and costs. He was born in Oswego County, New York, January 31st, 1836. He was baptized when ten years old, his family being already in the Church, when on the way from Nauvoo, with the exodus, to Winter Quarters, in 1846. He came to Utah in 1851 and settled in Fillmore. He is a farmer and stockraiser. He is a large man, being over six feet in height, and long featured.

JAMES E. TWICHEL; unlawful cohabitation; plea of not guilty. He had two trials, the jury having hung on the first, but were unanimous for conviction on the second. He was sentenced, by Judge Boreman, December 22nd, 1885; term, six months; fine, $300 and costs. He was born near Lacomb, Illinois, October 19th, 1854, and came to Utah in 1848. He left the Territory and went to California in 1849 and returned in 1858. He settled on Indian Creek, near Beaver, and has resided there ever since.

DAVID M. STUART; unlawful cohabitation; plea of guilty; sentenced, by Judge O. W. Powers, January 4th, 1885; term, six months; fine, $300 and costs. He was born in Irvine, Ayrshire, Scotland, March 8th, 1826; baptized at Paisley, May 5th, 1842; came to America in 1845, and reached Utah in 1847. He has been on five missions to the States, and one to Great Britain. He is an old resident of Ogden. He is of medium height, rather long face, and promineht features.

JAMES H. NELSON; unlawful cohabitation; plea of guilty; sentenced, by Judge O. W. Powers, January 8th, 1886; term, six months; fine, $300 and costs. He was born at Jacksonville, Morgan County, Illinois, March 28th, 1839, his parents being at that time in the Church. He was baptized at the age of eight years, and was in Nauvoo in his childhood, and left there at the time of the general expulsion of the Saints. He came to Utah in September, 1852, and has resided there permanently. He is a real estate agent. He is short of stature, round and stout. His complexion is fair, and his face large.

WILLIAM WALLACE WILLEY; unlawful cohabitation; plea of guilty; sentenced February 10th, 1886, by Judge Zane; term, five months; fine, $200 and costs. He was born in Hancock County, Illinois, October 20th, 1841, his parents being then in the Church. The family removed to Nauvoo, and were expelled with the main body of the Saints. They were very destitute at Council' Bluffs, yet William's father was drafted into the Mormon Battalion and accompanied it on its eventful expedition. William came to Utah in 1851, and has ever since resided at Bountiful. His case was the first of its class from Davis County. His height is five feet nine inches, and his build is heavy. His complexion is medium, face, head, and features round.

JOHN PENMAN; polygamy; plea of not guilty; sentenced, by Judge Zane, February 10th, 1886; term, two years; fine, $25 and costs. He was born at Crossgates, near Dumfermline, Scotland, February 1st, 1835. He was baptized in July, 1862. He came to Utah in 1863; is a resident of Bountiful, Davis County, and follows the business of market gardener and farmer. He is over the medium height, bony and slender; has dark eyes and complexion.

ROBERT MORRIS; unlawful cohabitation; plea of guilty; sentenced, February 15th, 1886, by Judge Zane; term, six months; fine, $150 and costs. He was born at Barrowden, Rutland, England. His mother being already in the Church, he was baptized November 28th, 1852. Hè came to the United States in 1860, and re- sided in Cincinnati one year, coming to Utah in 1861. He is a resident of Salt Lake City, and by trade a tanner, being a member of a thrifty firm doing business in that line. He has been Counselor to Bishop McRae, of the Eleventh

Ward, since August, 1877. He is of slender build, but large of stature, his height being six feet two inches. His complexion is fair, and features unusually prominent, and his eyes are full, kindly, and expressive.

JOHN BOWEN; unlawful cohabitation; plea of not guilty; testified against himself; sentenced, by Judge Zane, February 17th, 1886; term, six months; fine, $300 and costs. He was born at Abersychan, Wales, September 12th, 1841, and joined the Church in 1853; came to Utah in 1862; resided in Salt Lake City four years and in Tooele for the last twenty years. He is by trade a gardener, besides being a musician, both in the vocal and instrumental branches of the art. His height is five feet eight inches; his hair and eyes are dark and complexion sallow. He is of spare build, and his features are long. He helped to lighten the hours of imprisonment by teaching the divine art to a number of convicts organized into a choir, which occasionally assisted, in a musical capacity, at the Sunday religious services.

THOMAS BURNINGHAM; unlawful cohabitation; plea of not guilty; sentenced, by Judge Zane,

February 17th, 1886; term, six months; fine, $300 and costs. He was born at Farnham, Surrey, England, September 18th, 1842; joined the Church in 1857; came to Utah in 1860, and settled in Bountiful, Davis County. He follows the business of market gardener.

W. G. SAUNDERS; unlawful cohabitation; two indictments; arraigned on one; plea of guilty; sentenced February 16th, 1886, by Judge O. W. Powers; term, six months; fine, $25 and costs. He was born at Soham, Cambridgeshire, England, January 10th, 1819; joined the Church in 1852; came to the United States, stayed in St. Louis one year, and came to Utah in 1854. He is a resident of Weber County. He is short of stature and stout build. On Wednesday, May 19th, 1886, having been taken out of the penitentiary to Ogden on purpose, he was arraigned on the second indictment, and pleaded guilty. Judge Powers imposed an additional penalty of six months' imprisonment.

SAMUEL H. B. SMITH; unlawful cohabitation; plea of not guilty; sentenced February 20th, 1886, by Judge Zane; term, six months; fine, $300 and costs. He was born at Shady Grove,

9

Davis County, Missouri, in 1838, and is the son of Samuel Smith and nephew of the Prophet Joseph. A few days after his birth the family were driven out of their home by a mob, the consequence being that his mother, owing to the exposure endured under such critical circumstances, contracted a severe illness from which she never recovered. Samuel spent his early childhood in Nauvoo, Illinois, from whence he was driven at the time of the general expulsion. He came to Utah with the Church in 1848. He is of prodigious size, being six feet two inches in height, and turns the scales at two hundred and fifty pounds. His physical strength is commensurate to his bulk. His complexion is fair, and his features are large.

JOSEPH MCMURRIN; unlawful cohabitation; plea of not guilty. The defendant took the stand and testified against himself. Sentenced, by Judge Zane, February 23rd, 1886; term, six months; fine, $300 and costs. He was born July 14th, 1821, near Glasgow, Scotland, and joined the Church in 1854. He came to Utah in 1856, and suffered considerable hardship on the journey over the plains. His height is five feet ten inches, and his build is square and heavy.

His features are broad, complexion fair, with blue eyes. He is a cooper by trade, but has not worked at that business for a good many years. He is the embodiment of honesty and sincerity.

HENRY DINWOODEY; unlawful cohabitation; plea of guilty; sentenced, by Judge Zane, February 23rd, 1886; term, six months; fine, $300 and costs. He was born at Warrington, England, September 11th, 1825. He joined the Church in 1847; emigrated to America in 1849. He stopped six months at New Orleans, and after that, until 1852, at St. Louis, when he came to Utah. He has pursued the business of manufacturing and dealing in furniture, and has taken the lead in those lines, there being no establishment in Utah to be compared to his in extent. He is five feet ten inches in height, and of full habit. His complexion is fair and eyes blue. His head and face are large; the features being somewhat rounded, rather than sharp.

AMOS MAYCOCK; unlawful cohabitation; defendant declined to plead; court entered a plea of not guilty for him. He took the stand and testified against himself. Sentenced, by Judge Powers, February 25th, 1886; term, five months;

fine, $100 and costs. He was born at a hamlet, called Ashorne, in Warwickshire, England, May 1st, 1836; joined the Church in 1848 ; emigrated to Council Bluffs in 1849, and came to Utah in 1852. He lived at Springville six years, and the remainder of the time of his residence in Utah, at North Ogden. He is a farmer. He is conspicuous, because of his size, being six feet three inches high, and of ponderous frame. His weight is about two hundred pounds. He has a large head, and an unusually long face, the features tending, of course, in the same direction. His hair and beard, when the latter is allowed to appear, are red, or of that color sometimes denominated sandy. On Wednesday, May 19th, 1886, while serving his term on the first conviction, he was arraigned in the First District Court, at Ogden, on the second indictment. The proceedings resulted in the imposition of another sentence to imprisonment for six months, by Judge Powers.

HELON H. TRACY ; unlawful cohabitation ; three indictments, tried on one; plea of not guilty. He took the witness' stand and testified against himself. He was sentenced February 25th, 1886, by Judge Powers, who said on the occasion: "There is no power on, under, or above the earth that can stop these prosecutions." Term, six months; fine, $300 and costs. He was born at Council Bluffs, Iowa, February 25th, 1849, his parents being in the Church at the time, and among those who were expelled from Nauvoo. He came to Utah in 1850, and has resided in Weber County ever since, with the exception of a few months. His height is five feet ten inches, and build slender. His complexion is fair, and features small; hair sandy. His trade is carpenter. He was taken to Ogden on May 19th, 1886, while serving his term in the penitentiary, arraigned on the second indictment, resulting in Judge Powers inflicting another sentence of imprisonment for six months. The inhumanity of the proceeding is intensified by the fact that Brother Tracy is an invalid, suffering from consumption.

CHARLES H. GREENWELL; unlawful cohabitation; plea of not guilty; testified against himself. Sentenced, by Judge Powers, February 25th, 1886; term, six months; fine, $300 and costs. His parents were in the Church at the time of his birth, which occurred at Philadelphia, Pennyslvania, October 28th, 1856. He came to Utah in 1859.

He has been engaged in the butcher business with his father. He is six feet in height, and of spare build; his complexion is dark and features sharp.

HUGH S. GOWANS; unlawful cohabitation; plea of not guilty; he testified against himself; sentenced February 26th, 1886, by Judge Zane; term, six months; fine, $300 and costs. There being three indictments, two were held over for future use. He was born in Perth, Scotland, in February, 1832, and joined the Church in August, 1850; came to Utah in 1855, and has ever since resided in Tooele County, being now President of the Stake known by that name. He has occupied at different times the position of Probate Judge, Deputy County Clerk, Deputy Recorder, and telegraph operator. He is of medium height and proportionate build. His hair and complexion are dark.

WILLIAM HENRY LEE; unlawful cohabitation; plea of not guilty; took the stand and testified against himself; sentenced February 26th, 1886, by Judge Zane; term, six months; fine, $300 and costs. He was born of Latter-day Saint parents, at Liberty, Clay County, Missouri, August 9th, 1836. The family passed through all the terrible persecutions in Missouri and in Nauvoo, which place they left at the time of the expulsion. He came to Utah in 1850, and has been a continuous resident of Tooele County ever since. He is a farmer; is six feet in height, and tips the scales at two hundred and forty pounds, his frame being unusually large, as are also his head and face. His hair and complexion are dark. He has been Sheriff of Tooele County.

HERBERT J. FOULGER; unlawful cohabitation; three indictments, but tried on one only, the two others being held in reserve. Plea of not guilty; testified against himself; sentenced February 26th, 1886, by Judge Zane; term, six months; fine, $300. He was born in London, England, January 10th, 1848; joined the Church October 23rd, 1862, and came to Utah in 1863. He has followed the trade of carpenter, book-keeper, and has been more lately superintendent of a co-operative store. He has been for a number of years a Counselor in the Bishopric of the Twenty-first Ward, Salt Lake City. He is short of stature and stout build. His hair and complexion are fair.

JOHN P. BALL; unlawful cohabitation; plea
of not guilty; supplied the testimony for self-
conviction; sentenced, by Judge Zane, February
27th, 1886; term, six months; fine, $300 and
costs. He was born at Claughton, Leicestershire,
England, October 4th, 1828; joined the Church
in 1860; came to Utah in 1862. He is somewhat
tall and spare, and complexion dark. He is a
resident of Salt Lake City.

THOMAS C. JONES; unlawful cohabitation; three
indictments, tried on one, the others being held
in reserve; plea of not guilty; testified against
himself; sentenced, by Judge Zane, February
27th, 1886; term, six months; fine, $300 and
costs. He was born in Birmingham, England,
February 11th, 1825; joined the Church October
25th, 1848; came to Utah in 1868. He is a brush-
maker; is short of stature, and fair complexion.

JOHN Y. SMITH; unlawful cohabitation; three
indictments, tried on one; plea of not guilty;
regular trial; sentenced February 27th, 1886, by
Judge Zane; term, six months; fine, $300 and
costs. He was born at Johnston, Renfrewshire,
Scotland, October 20th, 1833; joined the Church
in 1852, and came to Utah in 1857, in a hand

cart company, under the supervision of Captain Raleigh, of American Fork. He has been a member of the Salt Lake City police force since 1869. He has held the position of Counselor in the Third Ward Bishopric since 1877. His height is five feet ten inches, and his build is square and heavy. Complexion sandy.

. JAMES MOYLE; unlawful cohabitation; three indictments, tried on one; plea of not guilty; testified against himself; sentenced March 1st, 1886, by Judge Zane; term, six months; fine, $300 and costs. He was born at Rosemeln, Cornwall, England, October 31st, 1835; joined the Church in February, 1852, at Devonport, England; came to Utah in 1854. He is a mason, and is foreman of the builders and stonecutters on the Temple Block, Salt Lake City. His height is five feet ten inches; complexion dark. Before his incarceration his face was adorned with a handsome flowing beard.

GEORGE H. TAYLOR; unlawful cohabitation; three indictments, tried on one; supplied the testimony to convict by going upon the witness stand; sentenced, by Judge Zane, March 1st, 1886; term, six months; fine, $300 and costs.

He was born at Bloomfield, Essex County, N. Y., November 4th, 1829; joined the Church at Haverstraw, Rockland County, N. Y., September 22nd, 1848; came to Utah in 1859. He has been Counselor in the Bishopric of the Fourteenth Ward for a number of years. He is rather short of stature and spare build. His complexion is dark. He is a lumber merchant, wood-worker, etc., and has an excellent reputation for business energy and ability. He is senior member of the firm of Taylor, Romney & Armstrong.

O. F. DUE; unlawful cohabitation; plea of guilty; sentenced March 1st, 1886, by Judge Zane; term, six months; fine, $300 and costs. He was born at Slemminge, Maribo County, Denmark, September 15th, 1836; joined the Church in 1869; came to Utah in 1872. His height is medium and complexion fair. He is a gardener.

JAMES O. POULSON; unlawful cohabitation; three indictments, tried on one; plea of guilty; sentenced, by Judge Zane, March 1st, 1886; term, six months; fine, $300 and costs. He was born at Malma, Sweden, July 7th, 1826;

joined the Church in 1871, and came to Utah the same year. He is a farmer; height medium: complexion dark; build rather stout; face and features round; resident of West Jordan.

SAMUEL F. BALL; unlawful cohabitation; three indictments, tried on one; plea of not guilty: testified against himself; sentenced March 1st, 1886, by Judge Zane; term, six months; fine, $300 and costs. He was born at Stockcross, Berks, England, April 14th, 1849; joined the Church July 6th, 1877; came to Utah in 1881; he is short and spare; complexion light; face somewhat thin. He is by trade a confectioner.

HYRUM GOFF; unlawful cohabitation; three indictments, tried on one; plea of not guilty: supplied the testimony for his own conviction; sentenced by Judge Zane, March 3rd, 1886; term, six months; fine, $300 and costs. He was born at Longwhatton, Leicestershire, England, July 29th, 1849, his parents being then in the Church; came to Utah in 1862. He is about five feet seven inches in height, has brown hair, brownish grey eyes, and florid complexion. He is of rather slender build and genteel appearance. He is a resident of West Jordan.

WILLIAM JENKINS; unlawful cohabitation; two indictments, tried on one; plea of not guilty; supplied the testimony for the prosecution from his own lips; sentenced March 3rd, 1886, by Judge Zane; term, six months; fine, $300 and costs. He was born in Nauvoo, Hancock County, Illinois, September 1st, 1841, his parents being in the Church; driven out at the time of the general expulsion; came to Utah in 1863. His height is about five feet eight inches; hair, light brown; complexion, florid; build strong and square; farmer; resident of West Jordan.

FREDERICK A. COOPER; unlawful cohabitation; three indictments, tried on one; plea of not guilty; voluntarily supplied the testimony for the prosecution; sentenced March 8th, 1886, by Judge Zane. He was born at Godmanchester, Huntingdonshire, England; joined the Church in 1849, his parents being already connected with it. He came to Utah in 1859 in a hand cart company, and pulled one of those vehicles over the plains. His height is five feet eight inches; hair brown, complexion unusually florid; eyes, grey. His-build is stout, inclining to corpulency. He has followed the mercantile business, but the prosecution breaks him up.

JOHN W. SNELL; unlawful cohabitation; three indictments, tried on one; plea of not guilty; regular trial; sentenced March˙ 9th, 1886, by Judge Zane; term, six months; fine, $300 and costs.

[For declining to answer certain questions propounded by Commissioner McKay, examining magistrate, and subsequently by the grand jury, Eliza Shafer, Mr. Snell's plural wife, was sent to the penitentiary in September, 1885, and remained there imprisoned over three months. At the trial she signified her willingness to go to the Detroit House of Correction for a term of years, an alternative threatened by the court, for the same reason. At the request of her husband, however, she answered the questions.]

John W. Snell was born at La Harpe, Hancock County, Illinois, March 2nd, 1842. His mother being in the Church while he was in boyhood, he became a member at an early age; came to Utah in 1857, and has principally resided in Salt Lake City. His height is five feet six inches; heavy build, large face and features; blueish grey eyes. In conversation his utterance is unusually rapid, and he has a notable faculty of touching upon a good many branches of a subject in a surprisingly brief space of time. He has the reputation of being greatly given to trading, that being his principal occupation.

LORENZO SNOW, one of the Twelve Apostles of the Church, entered the penitentiary March 12th, 1886. Three indictments having been found against him by the grand jury of the First District Court, for unlawful cohabitation, he plead not guilty to each. There were three regular trials, conviction being the result in each case. He was sentenced by Judge O. W. Powers, January 16th, 1886, the judgment being the full penalty of the law—imprisonment for six months and a fine of $300 and costs under each conviction. The defendant took an appeal to the Territorial Supreme Court and was in the meantime allowed to remain at large under bonds. The decision of the Territorial Supreme Court confirmed the judgment of the lower court, Chief Justice Zane concurring with Associate Justices Boreman and Powers in the first case, but dissenting from them in the other two. The two Associate Justices held that unlawful cohabitation was proved—in the absence of any other evidence—when it was shown that the defendant had lived with a plural wife while he had a legal wife living and undivorced. They held that the law presumed the living with the legal wife. In this view Judge Zane did not concur. The defendant took an appeal to the Supreme Court of the United States. In order to have the cases advanced upon the calendar of the court of last resort, it was necessary that he should be in durance. For the benefit of many of his brethren who had been indicted and others who were likely to be under the "segregating" process, he elected to go to prison to have the question of the right of the lower courts to so construe and administer the law, and other points, tested as early as practicable. The cases were argued and submitted, and, on May 10th, 1886, the U. S. Supreme Court dismissed the cases for want of jurisdiction. To make a show of consistency it reconsidered its own decision in the case of Angus M. Cannon, formerly disposed of, repealed its mandate therein, and treated it in the same fashion, as it belonged to the same class of cases as those of Lorenzo Snow.

Apostle Lorenzo Snow was born April 3rd, 1814, at Mantua, Portage County, Ohio, and was consequently on the verge of seventy-two years of age when he entered the prison. He joined the Church in June, 1836, at Kirtland, Ohio, and came to Utah in the fall of 1848. His place of residence is Brigham City, Box Elder County.

He is about five feet ten inches in height, and of somewhat spare build, his normal weight being one hundred and sixty pounds. His complexion is unusually dark ; his features exquisitely modelled, his countenance beaming with in. telligence. His manner is affable and refined, those who come in contact with him being at once impressed with the fact that he is a gentleman and a scholar. He has done a noble work . in connection with the Church. It is not intended to give any of the details of it here. They are published elsewhere. We, however, annex the speech made by him in the District Court, when he appeared before the judge to receive sentence.

On being asked whether he had anything to say why sentence should not be passed, upon him, Brother Snow read the following :

"Your honor, I wish to address this court kindly, respectfully, and especially without giving offense. During my trials, under three indictments, the court has manifested courtesy and patience, and I trust your honor has still a liberal supply, from which your prisoner at the bar indulges the hope that further exercise of those happy qualities may be anticipated. In the first place the court will please allow me to express my thanks and gratitude to my learned attorneys for their able and zealous efforts in conducting my defense.

"In reference to the prosecuting attorney, Mr. Bierbower, I pardon him for his ungenerous expressions, his apparent false coloring, and seeming abuse. The entire lack of evidence in the case against me on which to argue, made that line of speech the only alternative in which to display his eloquence; yet, in all his endeavors, he failed to cast more obloquy on me than was heaped upon our Savior.

"I stand in the presence of this court a loyal, free-born American citizen; now, as ever, a true advocate of justice and liberty. 'The land of the free, and the home of the brave,' has been the pride of my youth and the boast of my riper years. When abroad in foreign lands, laboring in the interest of humanity, I have pointed proudly to the land of my birth as an asylum for the oppressed.

"I have ever felt to honor the laws and institutions of my country, and, during the progress of my trials, whatever evidence has been introduced, has shown my innocence. But, like ancient Apostles when arraigned in Pagan courts, and in the presence of apostate Hebrew judges, though innocent, they were pronounced guilty. So myself, an Apostle who bears witness by virtue of his calling and the revelations of God, that Jesus lives—that He is the Son of God; though guiltless of crime, here in a Christian court I have been convicted through the prejudice and popular sentiment of a so-called Christian nation.

"In ancient times the Jewish nation and the Roman empire stood *versus* the Apostles. Now, under an apostate Christianity, the United

10

States of America stands *versus* Apostle Lorenzo Snow.

"Inasmuch as frequent reference has been made to my Apostleship, by the prosecution, it becomes proper for me to explain some essential qualifications of an Apostle.

"First, an Apostle must possess a Divine knowledge, by revelation from God, that Jesus lives—that He is the Son of the living God.

"Secondly, he must be divinely- authorized to promise the Holy Ghost; a divine principle that reveals the things of God, making known His will and purposes, leading into all truth, and showing things to come, as declared by the Savior.

"Thirdly, he is commissioned by the power of God to administer the sacred ordinances of the Gospel, which are confirmed to each individual by a divine testimony. Thousands of people now dwelling in these mountain vales, who received these ordinances through my administrations, are living witnesses of the truth of this statement.

"As an Apostle, I have visited many nations and kingdoms, bearing this testimony to all classes of people—to men in the highest official stations, among whom may be mentioned a President of the French republic. I have also presented works embracing our faith and doctrine to Queen Victoria and the late Prince Albert, of England.

"Respecting the doctrine of plural or celestial marriage, to which the prosecution so often referred, it was revealed to me, and afterwards, in

1843, fully explained 'to me by Joseph Smith, the Prophet.

" I married my wives because God commanded it. The ceremony, which united us for time and eternity, was performed by a servant of God having authority. God being my helper, I would prefer to die a thousand deaths than renounce my wives and violate these sacred obligations.

" The prosecuting attorney was quite mistaken in saying 'the defendant, Mr. Snow, was the most scholarly and brightest light of the Apostles ;' and equally wrong when pleading with the jury to assist him and the 'United States of America,' in convicting Apostle Snow, and he 'would predict that a new revelation would soon follow, changing the Divine law of celestial marriage." Whatever fame Mr. Bierbower may have secured as a lawyer, he certainly will fail as a prophet. The severest prosecutions have never been followed by revelations changing a divine law, obedience to which brought imprisonment or martyrdom.

" Though I go to prison, God will not change his law of celestial marriage. But the man, the people, the nation, that oppose and fight against this doctrine and the Church of God will be overthrown.

" Though the Presidency of the Church and the Twelve Apostles should suffer martyrdom, there will remain over four thousand Seventies, all Apostles of the Son of God, and were these to be slain there still would remain many thousands of High Priests, and as many or more Elders, all possessing the same authority to administer Gospel ordinances.

" In conclusion, I solemnly testify, in the name of Jesus, the so-called 'Mormon Church' is the Church of the living God; established on the rock of revelation, against which 'the gates of hell cannot prevail.'

" Thanking your honor for your indulgence, I am now ready to receive my sentence."

ABRAM H. CANNON; unlawful cohabitation; plea, not guilty: testified against himself rather than his family should be compelled to be witnesses for the prosecution. He was sentenced March 17th, 1886, by Judge C. S. Zane; term, six months; fine, $300 and costs. He made a speech in court, expressing his determination not to make any agreement to cast away his family or renounce a principle of his religion. He was born March 12th, 1859, in Salt Lake City, where he resides. His business is printer and publisher, besides engaging to some extent in literature. His height is five feet ten inches and proportionate build. His face is large, intelligent, and kindly, and complexion light. He is a son of President George Q. Cannon, and one of the Seven Presidents of Seventies. He filled a mission to Europe, partly to England and the remainder in the Swiss and German mission. While abroad he acquired the German language.

ROBERT McKENDRICK; unlawful cohabitation; two indictments; plea of guilty to one indictment and not guilty to the other. Sentenced March 18th, 1886, by Judge Zane, Third Judicial District; term, six months; fine, $300 and costs. He was born August 26th, 1828, at Kinboo, Antrim County, Ireland; joined the Church December 12th, 1852, and came to Utah in 1859. He is a resident of Tooele, and is by trade a butcher. His stature is five feet four inches, and his build is heavy, his weight being two hundred and fifteen pounds. His complexion is light.

LORENZO D. WATSON; unlawful cohabitation: three indictments, tried on one; plea of not guilty. The defendant supplied the testimony by going upon the stand himself for the prosecution, acknowledging his wives in that relationship, and admitting that he had lived with them. He was sentenced, by Judge J. S. Boreman, March 25th, 1886; term, six months; fine, $300 and costs. He was born in Limerick, York County, Maine, September 17th, 1845; joined the Church in July, 1868, and came to Utah the same year. He is a resident of Parowan, Iron County, and follows the legal profession. His height is nearly six feet, and build spare, his normal weight being one hundred and forty-five pounds. His complexion is light.

WILLIAM GRANT; unlawful cohabitation; two indictments, tried on one; plea of not guilty; took the stand for the prosecution against himself, acknowledging his wives and that he had lived with them; sentenced April 13th, 1886, by Judge O. W. Powers; term, four months. He was born at Willenhall, Staffordshire, England December 25th, 1838; joined the Church in 1851, and came to Utah in 1866. He is a resident of American Fork, was trained in the trade of locksmith, and is a professional music teacher. He is short of stature, being only five feet four inches in height, and of spare build, his usual weight being one hundred and twenty-five pounds. His complexion is medium.

NEPHI J. BATES; unlawful cohabitation; plea of not guilty; took the stand for the prosecution against himself; sentenced, by Judge O. W. Powers, April 13th, 1886; term, three months; fine, one dollar and costs (the costs amount to $293.70). He was born in New Orleans, Louisiana, November 18th, 1848; his parents being then in the Church he was reared in the faith. He came to Utah in 1852, and is a resident of Monroe, Sevier County. His profession is telegraphing. He is five feet nine inches in stature, and of medium build, his weight being one hundred and forty-eight pounds. His complexion is light.

JOHN BERGEN; unlawful cohabitation; two indictments, one having four counts; plea of not guilty; regular trials; convicted on both; sentence on indictment with one count still pending. Sentenced by Judge Zane, April 26th, 1886; term, six months on each count (two years), and $300 and costs (aggregating $1,200 and costs). Is also under indictment for polygamy. He was born in Christianstad, Sweden, June 22nd, 1822; joined the Church in June, 1855; a resident of Salt Lake City, and by trade a tailor.

STANLEY TAYLOR; unlawful cohabitation; four indictments, tried on one, the others pending; plea of not guilty; testified against himself by admitting the relationship between himself and his wives, and his having lived with them in that association. Sentenced May 10th, 1886, by Judge Zane; term, six months; fine, $300 and costs. He was born January, 1838, at Bolton, Lancashire, England; joined the Church Novcmber 21st, 1853; came to Utah September, 1860. He is a resident of Salt Lake City, and follows the business of hack proprietor and driver. He is short of stature and heavy build. His complexion is light.

GEORGE B. BAILEY; unlawful cohabitation; one indictment; plea of not guilty; regular trial; sentenced May 10th, 1886, by Judge Zane; term, six months; fine, $300 and costs. He was born February 15th, 1833, in Bath, England; joined the Church in May, 1851; came to Utah in 1853, and resides at Mill Creek, Salt Lake County. He is by trade a cabinet maker; but does not follow that pursuit, being employed in farming and bee culture. He is in stature within one inch of being six feet, and of spare build, his normal weight being about one hundred and sixty pounds. His complexion is light.

ANDREW JENSEN; unlawful cohabitation; plea of not guilty; had a regular trial; sentenced May 10th, 1886, by Judge Zane; term, six months; fine, $300 and costs. He was born March 8th, 1841, in Raadved, Denmark; joined the Church in 1863; came to Utah in 1867; and is a resident of Mill Creek, Salt Lake County.

He is a farmer. His stature is five feet nine inches, and his build medium; complexion light.

HENRY W. NAISBITT; unlawful cohabitation; three indictments, tried on one (the first); plea of not guilty; regular trial. He requested to be given some time between conviction and sentence, to enable him to arrange his business so that his family might not have to suffer during his absence from them. Prosecuting Attorney Dickson opposed the granting of the request, saying that he was tired of such delays. The court thereupon used its discretion in declining to accede to the solicitation of the defendant. The latter was sentenced May 11th, 1886, by Judge Zane; term, six months; fine, $300 and costs. H. W. Naisbitt was born at Romanby, Yorkshire, England, November 7th, 1827; joined the Church in 1851; came to Utah in 1854. He is a resident of Salt Lake City, and has had many ups and downs in business, which has been chiefly in the mercantile line. Among other qualifications he possesses are those of being a facile writer and fluent speaker. His complexion is light, his hair and beard having been originally what is termed sandy, but are now somewhat whitened by the effects of time. His height is about five feet

eight inches, and build slender. In the fall of
1878 he returned from a mission to England, on
which he was absent about two years.

GEORGE C. LAMBERT; unlawful cohabitation.
There was one indictment against him, but it con-
tained three counts, during the time covered by
two of which (1883 and 1884) the defendant was
in England on a mission. On this fact being repre-
sented to the prosecuting attorney he agreed to
prosecute only on the third count, and asked that
the jury return a verdict of not guilty on the other
two. This was accordingly done. The defendant
pleaded not guilty, and, rather than permit his
family to be brought into court, gave evidence
against himself, acknowledging his relationship
with his wives, and having lived with them in
that association. He was sentenced May 11th,
1886, by Judge Zane; term, six months; fine
$300 and costs. Brother Lambert was born in
"Winter Quarters," April 11th, 1848, and came,
or rather was brought to Utah in 1849, and is a
resident of this city. He is a printer and journal-
ist by profession, having been for a year and a
half prior to his incarceration upon 'the editorial
staff of the *Deseret News*. He is over medium
height and stouter than the average build. His

complexion is light, and his features what might be termed round and full; the forehead rather high and broad. He is naturally resolute and courageous.

CHAPTER IV.

Conclusion.

THERE are some things in life that cannot be learned otherwise than by experience. Among these are the sensations produced by the process of being placed in prison. They undoubtedly vary according to circumstances and the constitution of the individual. In some of its aspects—with special reference to those involved in the present legal and judicial persecutions of the Latter-day Saints—it provides a graphic comparison to the passage through the "dark valley of the shadow of death."

The conviction, involving the certainty of departure from the outward world, stands side by side with the impression upon the mind of the stricken patient, who feels that his falling into the hands of the grim-visaged monster is inevit-

able. The departure of the victim for the prison
has also many concomitants in common with the
snuffing out of the lamp of life. There are weep-
ing loved ones, who mourn, with bursting hearts,
because of the temporary separation from him
who perhaps has been their chief earthly comfort,
reliance and source of strength. With him the
principal regret—which overtops all others—is
for those whom he leaves behind while he is
snatched from the presence of social and domestic
joys to suffer temporary death. There is the same
swelling of the heart and falling of the sym-
pathetic tear when the name of the absent one is
mentioned, and the vacant chair where he was
wont to sit is regarded with the same veneration
as if he had crossed the dark, deep river. There
is the same hope, in a less extended form, of a lov-
ing reunion when the prison doors shall open
and the captive be set free, that inspires the
deeply religious soul who looks, "as fond antici-
pation forward points the view," to the never fad-
ing glories of the resurrection and the renewal
in eternity of those sacred associations formed in
mortality, under the seal of divine recognition.

In the captive's mind, when he enters the por-
tals of the penitentiary, there is perhaps a corres-
ponding mental vagueness regarding the condi-

tions into which he is about to be ushered, there being an air of mystery in the minds of people in the outer world in relation to prison life. There is this difference: When the upright man whose conscience is void of offense toward God or man, is about to pass to the spirit land, there are no misgivings as to the betterment of the conditions, while no matter how righteous he may be, he steps upon the threshold of the prison with a feeling of mingled repugnance and misgiving, no matter how stout may be his heart, or resolute his purpose.

To the independent spirit the deprivation of liberty is bitter beyond expression. He can bear it quietly, nay submissively, but while there is the outward indication of calm subjection, who can tell the occasional surging within the sensitive soul who prizes freedom and fully senses the damning crime of those who unjustly placed him within the hated precincts of a jail designed for those alone who have outraged the laws of nature and of nature's God and whose incarceration is properly demanded for the protection of their fellow creatures? Surely an inward protest against such acts is not an offense against Omnipotence, for he who is for conscience' sake confined with felons and shut out from liberty says to himself:

"Peace, troubled soul—be still." And then: "Not my will be done, O God, but Thine."

But there are compensations for unjust punishment and indignities heaped upon the victims of a mistaken as well as cruel policy in the vain attempt to crush religious convictions out of the hearts of a devoted people. The thoughtful man, imprisoned for religion's sake, is above and beyond contamination by contact with the baser class of mortals. His liberty is taken, but while his body is held in bondage, no power can prevent his soul from soaring. He is thrown into close association with a phase of humanity of whom he has known comparatively nothing. No other condition could have brought about the intermingling—it had to be enforced. It never could have been induced by voluntary action. Yet who shall say that this intimacy with the lower degrees of humanity is not necessary to complete a fundamental experience requisite to form the basis of extensive sympathy, and a broadened range of thought? It is learned that many, if not all, unfortunate creatures have various redeeming traits. Circumstances call them out, when they shine like the broad lightning flashes that gleam over the horizon of a midnight sky. It is found that, in many cases, encouragement causes those bright scintillations to become more frequent, then less evanescent, until the conviction ensues that in most instances the heretofore latent spark which shed the transitory rays is susceptible of becoming, by judicious fanning, a steady flame.

This fact impresses the thoughtful man with the sublime truth that there is in every mortal, however infinitessimal it may be, a spark of divinity. If he love God, he will love him whom God so loves as to uphold him and maintain in his soul some degree of the light that emanates from Himself. A new lustre breaks in upon a keenly perceptive mind. The grand truth that God is the father and creator of all, has greater potency, and a deeper desire to be useful to the race is more firmly engendered.

He who gains this experience while in a sense maintaining a position above and beyond that which is most groveling, goes below it, in order that, with an increased understanding, he may soar more loftily above it. Heretofore he has only been familiar with the topography of the sphere of human life, now he digs deep, reaches the lower strata, comprehends the geological construction, and is thus better prepared to ascend and explore its astronomical or celestial aspects. With his new, deeper, and broader understanding he emerges better prepared for the battle of life, more fitted to take a firm, resolute stand for truth, and to lend an abler hand in bettering the condition of his fellow-creatures. The prison picture is not all gloom, for out of the darkness the light is seen in the great beyond, shining with increasing splendor.